Meet Lily Wong

She's not the girl next door... unless you happen to live on the 19th floor of a crumbling public housing estate across the street from a Kowloon cement factory.

She's Wong Lei Lei, a sweet, savvy, sassy young woman who loves her job, loves her family, and most of all loves Hong Kong. Amidst the screaming commotion of the colony, while everyone around her is scrambling for profits or clambering to emigrate, she struggles to lead a normal life.

But one day on the morning rush-hour train, she comes up against — literally — the man who will change her life...

Most of the cartoons in this book appeared previously in either the *Hongkong Standard* or the *South China Morning Post*.

©1988 Larry Feign

All rights reserved. No part of this publication, including text and/or artwork, may be reproduced, stored in a retrieval system, or transmitted, in any form or by any means, electronic, mechanical, photocopying, recording or otherwise, without the prior written permission of the publisher.

The characters and events depicted in this book are fictional. Any resemblance to actual persons, living or dead, is unintentional. Yes, that's right, it's not about me or my wife. I've never worked in an advertising agency and I pray I should never stoop so low. And my wife was never a secretary. In fact, she's a psychotherapist, and the next person who suggests that she is in fact Lily Wong may find him or herself involuntarily committed to Castle Peak!

First published 1988 by Macmillan Publishers (HK) Ltd

ISBN 962 7866 03 2

Published 1993 by

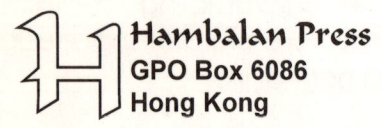

Hambalan Press
GPO Box 6086
Hong Kong

printed in the British Crown Colony of Hong Kong
second Hambalan printing, 1995

See "The World of Lily Wong"
on the Internet's World Wide Web!

http://www.asiaonline.net/lilywong

The World of Lily Wong

written and illustrated by
Larry Feign

edited by
**Cathy Sau Yung Tsang-Feign,
M.A., M.S., M.F.C.C.**

lettering by
Ivan Chan

This book is for

my mother and father,

who still think I would have made a better lawyer.

Contents

Some Enchanted Morning   (page 1)
Rudy Gets a Job   (page 19)
The Road to Ruin   (page 31)
Darling Lily   (page 47)
Washington Bound   (page 61)
Lily's Dilemma   (page 77)
All That Glitters   (page 99)
Farewell, My Lily   (page 115)
Epilogue   (page 123)

1 Some Enchanted Morning

SIGH! EVERY DAY THE SAME THING ON THIS DAMN MTR!
PACKED LIKE SARDINES, CAN'T BREATHE, SUIT GETS WRINKLED...
...AND I COME OUT SMELLING LIKE THE COLLECTIVE SWEAT OF 5½ MILLION PEOPLE! I HATE IT!!
...OF COURSE, THERE ARE ADVANTAGES...
FEIGN

WHAT LUCK! ON A CROWDED MTR, SQUEEZED UP AGAINST THE MOST BEAUTIFUL WOMAN IN HONG KONG!
I WISH I COULD THINK OF SOMETHING TO SAY...
EXCUSE ME...
WOW! SHE'S TALKING TO ME!!
YOU CAN QUIT LEANING ON ME NOW!
出口 EXIT
FEIGN

WHAT A BEAUTIFUL WOMAN! I'VE GOT TO TRY ASKING HER OUT!
ER... HELLO, MY NAME'S STUART. WHAT'S——
WHACK!!
I THOUGHT ALL CHINESE WOMEN WERE SHY AND DEMURE...
I THOUGHT ALL GWAILO WERE AS TOUGH AS RAMBO!
FEIGN

WILL YOU GO OUT WITH ME?
NO.
WHY NOT?
MY FAMILY WOULDN'T APPROVE.
YOUR PARENTS?
NO, MY HUSBAND!
FEIGN

YOU'RE NOT REALLY MARRIED, ARE YOU?
NO.
HAPPY LUCK GOLDEN FORT BRIGHTER SUC CO. LTD. 444
THEN WHY WON'T YOU GO OUT WITH ME?
BECAUSE YOU'RE A JERK!
OH WELL, I'LL JUST HAVE TO SHARE MY MILLION DOLLAR INHERITANCE WITH SOMEBODY ELSE!!
HAPPY LUCKY GOLDEN FORTUN BRIGHTER SUCC CO. LTD. 444
LILY 3-523011...
HAPPY LU GOLDEN FOR BRIGHTER S CO. LTD 444
FEIGN

DID YOU GIVE ME YOUR PHONE NUMBER JUST BECAUSE I CLAIMED TO HAVE A MILLION DOLLAR INHERITANCE?
HAPPY LUCK GOLDEN FORT BRIGHTER SU CO. LTD. 444
NO WAY! I'M NOT THAT KIND OF GIRL!
WHACK!
OH YEAH?? MOST LOCAL PEOPLE WOULD GIVE THEIR RIGHT ARM FOR A MILLION DOLLARS!!
NOT ME!
NOW, IF IT WERE **YEN**... OR **DEUTSCHMARKS**...
HAPP GOLD BRIGH C 4
FEIGN

MORNING, PIXIE!
YOU'RE *LATE*, MR. WRIGHT!!
YOU'RE LATE, STUART!
WRIGHT, YOU'RE 40 MINUTES LATE!
X.P. McGU Direct
SIGH! IT'S NICE TO KNOW WHEN YOU'RE MISSED!
FEIGN

STUART, A MAJOR CLIENT NEEDS A PROMOTION FOR THEIR NEW PRODUCT...
...A CIGARETTE AIMED AT THE 5-TO-10 YEAR OLD MARKET!
WHAT??!! BUT, MR. McGUFF... THAT'S *IMMORAL!!* THAT'S SHAMEFUL!! THAT'S **DISGUSTING!!!**
OF COURSE! AND SO IS THE AMOUNT WE'RE CHARGING THEM TO DO IT!
FEIGN

IT'S IMMORAL TO INFLUENCE YOUNG KIDS TO START SMOKING!!
BUT WE AREN'T!
OUR ADS ARE ONLY MEANT TO CONVINCE 5-TO-10 YEAR OLDS *WHO ARE ALREADY SMOKERS* TO SWITCH BRANDS!
YEAH, BUT NOT MANY KIDS THAT AGE HAVE TAKEN UP CIGARETTES.
WE'VE THOUGHT OF THAT...
...WHICH IS WHY WE'RE ALSO PASSING THEM OUT FREE OUTSIDE PRIMARY SCHOOLS AND PLAYGROUNDS!
FEIGN

ABOUT OUR NEW KIDDIE CIGARETTE ACCOUNT...
NO WAY! I REFUSE TO HELP!!
I ADMIRE YOU, STUART! A MAN WHO REFUSES TO COMPROMISE HIS PRINCIPLES!
THE WORLD WOULD BE BETTER OFF IF MORE PEOPLE FOLLOWED YOUR EXAMPLE!
THEN YOU'LL REFUSE THE CIGARETTE AD CONTRACT?
AND TURN DOWN $500,000?! THAT WOULD BE AGAINST **MY** PRINCIPLES!!
FEIGN

IT'S WRONG TO SELL CIGARETTES TO 5-TO-10 YEAR OLDS!!
STUART, THIS IS AN AD AGENCY...
...LEAVE IT TO THE PHILOSOPHERS TO DECIDE BETWEEN RIGHT AND WRONG, GOOD AND EVIL...
THE RIGHT AND GOOD THINGS WILL SURVIVE ON THEIR MERITS...
AND THE REST...?
THAT'S WHAT ADVERTISING IS FOR!
FEIGN

TO CALL OR NOT TO CALL?
AFTER ALL, I JUST MET HER ON THE MTR FOR 5 MINUTES!
WHAT IF I SOUND STUPID? WHAT IF SHE SECRETLY HATES FOREIGNERS?? WHAT IF SHE LAUGHS IN MY FACE??!
H-HELLO? L-L-LILY P-PLEASE?
SORRY, WRONG NUMBER!
WHEW!
THANK GOD!!
SLAM!
FEIGN

WAI...?
HELLO, MAY I—
click!
Grrrr...
WAI...?
HELLO, I'D—
click!
ALL RIGHT! HAVE IT YOUR WAY!!
WAI!!
WHO IS IT, MOTHER?
SOME STUPID FOREIGNER. HE JUST LEARNED THE WORD "WAI"!
FEIGN

WAI?
HELLO, MAY I PLEASE SPEAK TO LILY?
WAI?
LILY! I'D LIKE TO SPEAK TO LILY!
WAI?
LILY, DAMN IT!! LILY, YOU STUPID OLD WOMAN!! I WANT LILY! LILY! LILY!
SPEAKING...!
oops...
FEIGN

HELLO, LILY?
ER... YES. WHO'S THIS?
THIS IS STUART... REMEMBER ME?
WHO?
STUART WRIGHT. WE MET ON THE MTR!
WE DID?
YOU CALLED ME A STUPID JERK.
OH, THAT STUART! HOW ARE YOU!!
FEIGN

LILY, WILL YOU GO OUT TO DINNER WITH ME?
ONLY IF YOU MAKE IT THREE DINNERS!
TWO DINNERS, THEN.
TWO DINNERS AND A SHOW!
TWO DINNERS AND A LUNCH, AND THAT'S MY FINAL OFFER!!
IT'S A DEAL!
JEEZ, YOU HAVE TO BARGAIN FOR EVERYTHING IN HONG KONG!
FEIGN

HELLO ... CHEN? YOU'VE GOT TO HELP ME!!
I'M TAKING OUT THIS CHINESE WOMAN, BUT I DON'T KNOW WHAT TO GET HER...
A CORSAGE? A BOUQUET? CHOCOLATES?
WHAT WOULD A TYPICAL HONG KONG WOMAN LIKE TO RECEIVE ON A FIRST DATE??
Restaurant
FEIGN

WHEN YOU TOLD ME TO MEET YOU AT THIS RESTAURANT, I COULDN'T BELIEVE IT!
Restaurant
THIS IS THE FANCIEST PLACE IN TOWN! IT MUST COST A FORTUNE!!
Restaurant
THINK NOTHING OF IT...
...BECAUSE WE'RE EATING OVER THERE!
FEIGN

I LOVE EATING AT THESE DAAI PAAI DONGS...
記方
GREAT FOOD, UNBEATABLE PRICES, AND SUCH... SUCH...
...WELL, IN ENGLISH, WE DESCRIBE IT WITH A FRENCH WORD: *AMBIANCE*. WHAT WOULD YOU CALL IT IN CHINESE?
CHEAP!!
FEIGN

YOU SPEAK VERY GOOD ENGLISH!
THEN WHY DO YOU MENTION IT?
HUH?
I MEAN, IF MY ENGLISH WASN'T VERY GOOD, YOU'D SAY IT'S GOOD JUST TO ENCOURAGE ME...
...WHEREAS, IF MY ENGLISH IS REALLY SO GOOD, THEN IT'S REDUNDANT TO POINT IT OUT...
記方
...SO WHAT YOU'RE REALLY IMPLYING IS...
YOUR ENGLISH IS ***TOO*** *GOOD!*
FEIGN

I MEAN IT! YOUR ENGLISH IS QUITE GOOD!
WHY IS THAT SUPPOSED TO BE A COMPLIMENT WHEN IT'S REALLY JUST A FACT?!
I'M MERELY TRYING TO BE PLEASANT!
I MEAN, IT'S THE SAME AS IF YOU SAID I SPEAK GOOD CHINESE: IT'S OBVIOUSLY NOT TRUE, BUT YOU JUST SAY IT...
WHY DO I ALWAYS GET MYSELF INTO THIS?
FEIGN

DO YOU SPEAK CHINESE?
NOT A WORD!
HAVE YOU TRIED TO LEARN?
WHY BOTHER? EVERYONE HERE SPEAKS ENGLISH!
YOU'RE CRAZY! NOT THAT MANY PEOPLE HERE ARE TRULY BILINGUAL!
OH YEAH?? YOU'D HAVE TO BE PRETTY IGNORANT TO LIVE IN A PLACE LIKE HONG KONG AND KNOW ONLY ONE LANGUAGE!
ER... PERHAPS I SHOULD REPHRASE THAT...
FEIGN

WHY DO YOU FOREIGNERS ALWAYS EXPECT US TO KNOW ENGLISH, WHILE YOU DON'T LEARN CHINESE?
WHY NOT? ENGLISH IS THE UNIVERSAL LANGUAGE...
IT'S THE LANGUAGE OF COMMERCE, THE LANGUAGE OF DIPLOMACY AND TECHNOLOGY...
...WHY, THE BIBLE ITSELF IS WRITTEN IN ENGLISH!
黐鬼線!!
WHAT DID HE SAY?
FEIGN

WHAT WORK DO YOU DO?
I'M A SECRETARY.
OH? FOR WHAT KIND OF BUSINESS?
WELL, IT'S SORT OF AN UNDERGROUND BUSINESS.
REALLY?! WHAT? COUNTERFEIT DESIGNER CLOTHES? EMBARGOED WEAPONS TRADING? BOOTLEG COMPUTERS? ENDANGERED SPECIES?
NO, COFFINS.
FEIGN

YOU REALLY WORK FOR A COFFIN EXPORTER??
DO YOU FIND THAT SO STRANGE?
I'D NEVER THOUGHT ABOUT IT! IS THAT A PROFITABLE TRADE? HOW'S BUSINESS?
QUITE DEAD, ACTUALLY.
FEIGN
WHY DID YOU COME TO HONG KONG?
I COULDN'T FIND WORK IN MY OWN COUNTRY.
WHY NOT?
WELL, BACK HOME I DIDN'T HAVE THE RIGHT EXPERIENCE, THE RIGHT TRAINING, THE RIGHT TALENT, THE RIGHT CONNECTIONS...
SO WHAT GOT YOU SUCH A GOOD, HIGH-PAYING JOB HERE?
THE RIGHT SKIN COLOUR!
FEIGN

MAY I KISS YOU?
NO, I CAN'T!
WHY? ARE YOU SHY?
NO.
WORRIED ABOUT GERMS?
NO.
AFRAID TO KISS A GWAILO?
NO.
THEN WHY CAN'T YOU KISS ME?
OUR LIPS WON'T REACH!!
FEIGN

DAUGHTER, WHO IS THIS MAN YOU WENT OUT WITH?
JUST SOMEONE I MET.
IS HE SOMEONE I WOULD APPROVE OF?
I DOUBT IT, FATHER.
WHAT?!! TELL ME ABOUT HIM!!
WELL, HE ISN'T VERY SMART, DOESN'T MAKE MUCH MONEY, DOESN'T BATHE, IMPOLITE, UGLY, AWKWARD...
OH, IS THAT ALL? WHEW! FOR A MOMENT THERE, I THOUGHT YOU WERE GOING TO TELL ME HE'S A GWAILO!
FEIGN

FATHER, THE MAN I WENT OUT WITH IS A GWAILO!
WHAT?!!
MY DAUGHTER LET HERSELF GO OUT WITH AN UNCIVILISED HEATHEN BARBARIAN?!!
I'LL BET HE TRIED TO PUT HIS BIG HAIRY HANDS ALL OVER YOU ON THE FIRST DATE!
AS A MATTER OF FACT, HE DID NOT!
HMM, NOT A VERY TYPICAL GWAILO, THEN, IS HE?
UNFORTUNATELY NOT!
FEIGN

WHAT'S WRONG WITH MY GOING OUT WITH A FOREIGNER?
THEY'RE NOTHING BUT TROUBLE FOR US CHINESE!
DON'T YOU KNOW YOUR HISTORY?! THEY CAME HERE TO SELL OPIUM!
CHINESE PEOPLE BOUGHT IT!
THEY'RE IMPERIALISTS WHO STOLE A PIECE OF CHINA AND COLONISED IT!!
AND SINCE THEN, EVERY PERSON IN CHINA HAS WANTED TO MOVE HERE!
THEY DON'T GIVE MONEY TO THEIR PARENTS OR IN-LAWS!!!
AH, WE'RE FINALLY GETTING TO THE HEART OF THE MATTER...
FEIGN

HOW DARE YOU GO OUT WITH A GWAILO!! WAIT UNTIL YOUR MOTHER FINDS OUT!
MOTHER, YOUR DAUGHTER IS SEEING A FOREIGN DEVIL BARBARIAN!!
THAT'S NICE.
WHAT DO YOU MEAN 'THAT'S NICE'?!! IT'S A DISGRACE TO THIS FAMILY!!
OH. THEN THAT'S NOT SO NICE.
SEE?! YOU'RE BREAKING YOUR MOTHER'S HEART!!
WHATEVER YOUR FATHER SAYS...
FEIGN

IF YOU CONTINUE TO SEE THAT FAAN GWAI LO, I'LL DISOWN YOU!!
HA! HOW CAN YOU DO THAT?? I'M THE ONLY ONE IN THIS FAMILY WHO'S WORKING! WITHOUT ME, YOU'D ALL STARVE!
RACING
I SAID I'LL DISOWN YOU NOT YOU'LL DISOWN US!!
I'LL THINK ABOUT IT.
FEIGN

2 Rudy Gets a Job

MARK 6

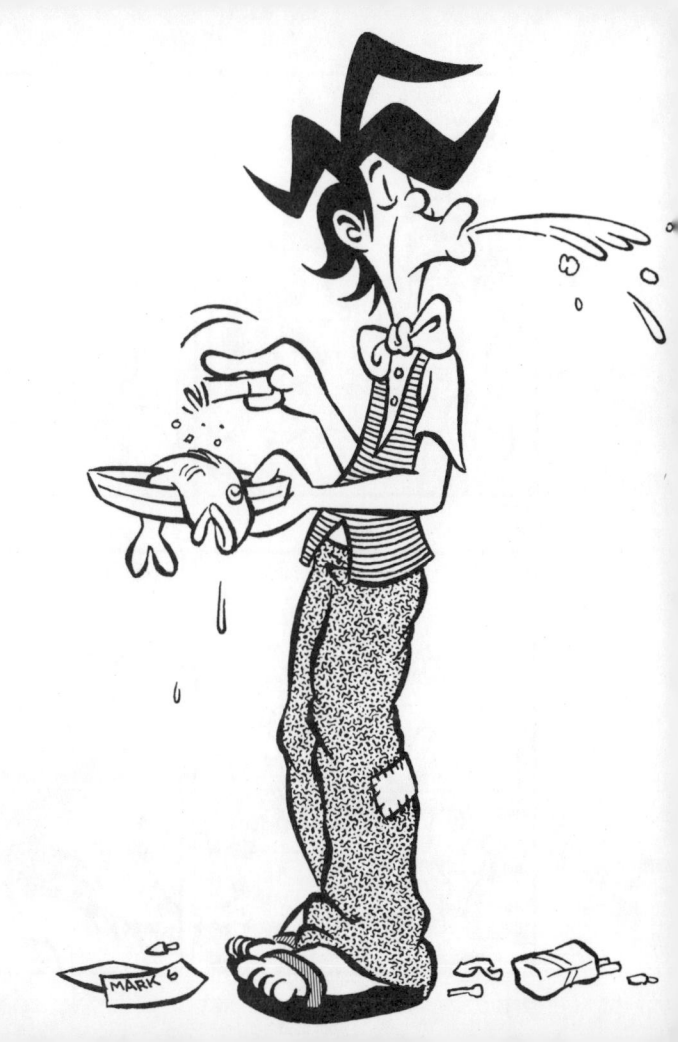

STILL GOING OUT WITH THAT GWAILO, SIS?
SORT OF.
GOOD. I NEED SOME MONEY FOR WEDNESDAY.
WHAT DOES MY SEEING A FOREIGNER HAVE TO DO WITH NEEDING MONEY?
WHY ELSE WOULD ANYONE GO OUT WITH A GWAILO??
MA! LILY SLUGGED ME!!
THAT'S NICE, DEAR.
FEIGN

IF YOU NEED MONEY, THEN GO GET A JOB!
MUK TAO NEWS
EASIER SAID THAN DONE.
WHAT DO YOU MEAN?
HAVEN'T YOU HEARD? THE UNEMPLOYMENT RATE IS OVER 10%! JOBS ARE SCARCER THAN GOLD!!
MUK TAO NEWS
JOBLESSNESS TOPS 10%
THAT'S IN THE U.K.!
DETAILS... DETAILS...
MUK TAO NEWS
JOBLESSNESS TOPS 10% IN NORTH WALES
FEIGN

HOW DO I FIND A JOB?
START BY LOOKING IN TODAY'S NEWSPAPER!
NORTH CHINA EVENING MAIL
HOURS GO BY...
SO? WHAT HAVE YOU COME UP WITH?
$20 ON GOLD DUST IN THE FIRST, $50 ON HANG LOOSE IN THE SECOND, $15 ON MYSTERY IN...
EVENING MAIL
RACING
Race 1
FEIGN

WHAT MAKES YOU WANT A JOB AS A WAITER?
DAAI DAAM RESTAURAN
MANAGER
WELL, I HAVE AN INTEREST IN GOURMET CUISINE, I LOVE TO WORK WITH PEOPLE, AND...
ALL RIGHT! I'M UNFIT FOR OTHER WORK AND I PLAN TO STEAL FOOD.
THAT'S BETTER. WE DON'T HIRE LIARS.
FEIGN

BEFORE I CAN HIRE YOU AS WAITERS, I HAVE TO GIVE YOU A MATHS TEST... WHAT'S 7 + 8?
DAAI DAAM RESTAURANT
MANAGER
15.
WRONG.
15.
WRONG.
22.
RIGHT! YOU'RE HIRED!
WHAT?! HOW COULD IT BE 22?? EVERYONE KNOWS THE ANSWER IS 15!!
YOU FORGOT THE $2 FOR MUSTARD, $3 FOR TEA, AND 10% SERVICE CHARGE!
FEIGN

GREAT NEWS!! I GOT A JOB AS A WAITER AT A FANCY RESTAURANT IN CENTRAL!
THAT'S WONDERFUL! NOW YOU'LL HAVE TO CUT YOUR HAIR, BATHE REGULARLY, WEAR CLEAN CLOTHES, STOP SMOKING, NOT USE FOUL LANGUAGE, BE POLITE, OBEY ORDERS, WEAR SHOES, BE PUNCTUAL, AND STOP PICKING YOUR NOSE!
THE NEXT DAY...
GET UP, RUDY! YOU'LL BE LATE FOR YOUR FIRST DAY OF WORK!
I QUIT. I COULDN'T TAKE THE PRESSURE.
RAMBO
FEIGN

GOOD MORNING, BOSS!
MORNING, LILY. YOU'RE 15 MINUTES LATE!
I'M SORRY, MR. NG, BUT WE'VE JUST HAD A LONG WEEKEND AND...
I'M SORRY, TOO! I'M AFRAID I'LL HAVE TO DOCK YOUR SALARY!
SO, LET'S SEE... 15 MINUTES... AT THE RATE I'M PAYING YOU... THAT SHOULD BE...
ABOUT 30¢, RIGHT?
NOT QUITE. BUT WE CAN ROUND IT UP TO THAT IF YOU LIKE.
FEIGN

LILY, WE'RE PUTTING TOGETHER OUR SPRING CATALOGUE OF COFFINS.
DISPLAY ROOM
THIS YEAR WE'RE AIMING AT THE YOUTH EXPORT MARKET, WITH OUR NEW LINE OF OFFICIAL SUPERSTAR "ROCKBOXES"!
ROD
ELTON
BUT, MR. NG, THOSE STARS AREN'T EVEN DEAD!
Mick
STING
PAUL
OH YEAH? HAVE YOU HEARD THEIR LATEST ALBUMS??
Iggy
FEIGN

LILY, WE NEED PICTURES FOR OUR SPRING COFFIN CATALOGUE. GO LIE DOWN IN THAT ONE.
AIEEYAAA!! NO WAY!!
YOU WANT TO LOSE YOUR JOB, BRINGING SHAME TO YOUR FAMILY??
SIGH... OK...
KNOCK KNOCK
SMILE! LET'S SEE SOME TEETH!
ER...EXCUSE ME, I'M LOOKING FOR MISS LILY WONG...
I JUST WANT TO ASK HER—
EEEEEK!!!
FEIGN

LILY!!! WHAT HAPPENED?! IT CAN'T BE TRUE!
BOO HOO HOO...
STUART! WHAT ARE YOU DOING HERE?
Y-YOU'RE ALIVE!!?
OF COURSE!
IN THAT CASE, HOW ABOUT GOING TO LUNCH WITH ME?
SORRY, I'M BUSY!
IN OTHER WORDS— YOU'D RATHER BE DEAD THAN BE WITH ME?
SOMETHING LIKE THAT.
FEIGN

COME ON, LILY, JOIN ME FOR LUNCH!
I TOLD YOU, I CAN'T! NOW PLEASE GO AWAY!
TSK! DON'T BE POLITE! I KNOW YOU CHINESE... ALWAYS SAYING "NO" WHEN YOU MEAN "YES". COME ON, LET'S GO!
FOR THE LAST TIME: NO!!!
WHACK!
THINK HE GOT THE HINT YET?
I DON'T KNOW. GWAILO AREN'T NOTED FOR THEIR SUBTLETY.
THWUMP!
FEIGN

STUART'S LOCKED IN THE COFFIN!
LET'S GO FIND A CROWBAR!
THIS THE SAMPLE FOR THE KAM NGAN FUNERAL PARLOUR?
MUST BE.
YOU HEAR SCREAMING?
PROBABLY THE BRAKES.
WHEW! THIS ONE'S HEAVY!
WOOPS!
CRUNCH!
YAAAA!!
AIEEYAAA! A GWAI*!!
LOOKS MORE LIKE A GWAILO!
FEIGN

*鬼 GHOST

IT'S YOUR FIRST DAY ON THE JOB. AS YOU KNOW, OUR RESTAURANT IS FAMOUS FOR ITS SERVICE!
JUST REMEMBER: THE CUSTOMERS ARE ALWAYS—
RIGHT!
DAAI DAAM RESTAURANT
NO, NITWIT! THE CUSTOMERS ARE ALWAYS **COMPLAINING!!** JUST IGNORE THEM!
TROUBLE MAKER!
FEIGN

WHICH WOULD YOU RECOMMEND?
WELL, #3 IS HIGHLY RATED...
MENU
...AND #18 ISN'T BAD, WHILE THE CHEF'S FAVOURITE IS #29, THOUGH PERSONALLY I'D GO FOR #12.
WOW! YOU REALLY KNOW THE FOOD HERE, DON'T YOU?
MENU
RACING TIPS
FOOD? WHAT FOOD?
MENU
FEIGN

BEAN SOUP?! BUT THE SET MEAL WE ORDERED COMES WITH SHARK'S FIN SOUP!
NO MORE SHARK FIN.
CHICKEN WINGS?!! BUT WE'RE SUPPOSED TO GET PRAWNS!
NO MORE PRAWN.
AND NOW **POTATOES** INSTEAD OF CHOI SUM?! *WHY DIDN'T YOU TELL US YOU WERE OUT OF EVERYTHING WHEN WE ORDERED?!!*
YOU DIDN'T ASK!

A-A-A-
CHOO
SMOKED FISH!

$132.
WHAT?! HOW COULD IT BE THAT MUCH??
$132
SEE? IT SAYS RIGHT HERE: SET MEAL FOR TWO... $80!
套餐
合兩位
八十元正
I KNOW, SIR...
...BUT YOU ORDER FROM *ENGLISH* MENU!
SET MEAL for 2 person $120
FEIGN

CHEN, WHY IS IT THAT ALL THE LOCAL GIRLS I MEET SEEM EITHER TO BE GOLDDIGGERS OR ARE COLD AS ICE TOWARD FOREIGNERS?
THAT'S AN UNFAIR RACIST STEREOTYPE!
THAT'S LIKE SAYING ALL EXPATRIATE MEN ARE LUST-CRAZED DRUNKEN HYENAS WHO CHEAT ON THEIR WIVES AND TRY TO TAKE ADVANTAGE OF ANY WOMAN WITH ASIAN FEATURES!
NOW, THAT'S *REALLY* UNFAIR, CHEN!
ASIAN FEATURES HAVE NOTHING TO DO WITH IT!!
FEIGN

CHEN, I DON'T GET IT! EVERY LOCAL WOMAN I'VE EVER GONE OUT WITH COMPLETELY REJECTS ME!
WHAT'S THE MATTER? DO ALL FOREIGNERS GET THE SAME TREATMENT OR AM I JUST A WIMP?
BRAD DAVIS HAS A CHINESE GIRLFRIEND, FRED LITTLE MARRIED ONE, ARNOLD STIEFELLECKER HAS FOUR CHINESE GIRLS AFTER HIM...
IT WAS A RHETORICAL QUESTION.
IT WAS A RHETORICAL ANSWER.
FEIGN

THE VEGETABLES HERE WERE ROTTEN, THE FISH WAS 3 WEEKS OLD...
THE SERVICE WAS NONEXISTENT AND THE PRICES OUTRAGEOUS...
THEN WHY DIDN'T YOU REFUSE TO LEAVE A TIP?
WHAT?? AND LOSE FACE?!
FEIGN

FORGET ABOUT LILY, STUART! INTERRACIAL RELATIONSHIPS RARELY WORK OUT ANYWAY!
WELL, THEY SHOULD! IF MORE RACES INTERMARRIED, THERE'D BE LESS HATE IN THE WORLD!!
THE TIMES
I SAY! I COULDN'T HELP BUT OVERHEAR. MY OWN DAUGHTER ONCE THOUGHT LIKE YOU AND HER MARRIAGE ENDED IN SHAMBLES AND DISGRACE.
U.K. IMMIGRATION SAYS NO TO VIETS, INDIANS,
AND ALL BECAUSE SHE MARRIED A MEMBER OF AN
OH? AND WHICH RACE WAS THAT?
ALIEN AND ARGUABLY UNCIVILISED RACE!
AMERICAN!
THE TIMES
FEIGN

SO HOW WAS YOUR FIRST WEEK OF WORK?
NOT BAD.
GOOD! HOW MUCH MONEY DID YOU TAKE HOME?
$15.
WHAT?! I THOUGHT THEY WERE SUPPOSED TO PAY YOU $500 PLUS A SHARE OF THE TIPS!!
THEY DID!
BET FORM
BET
FEIGN

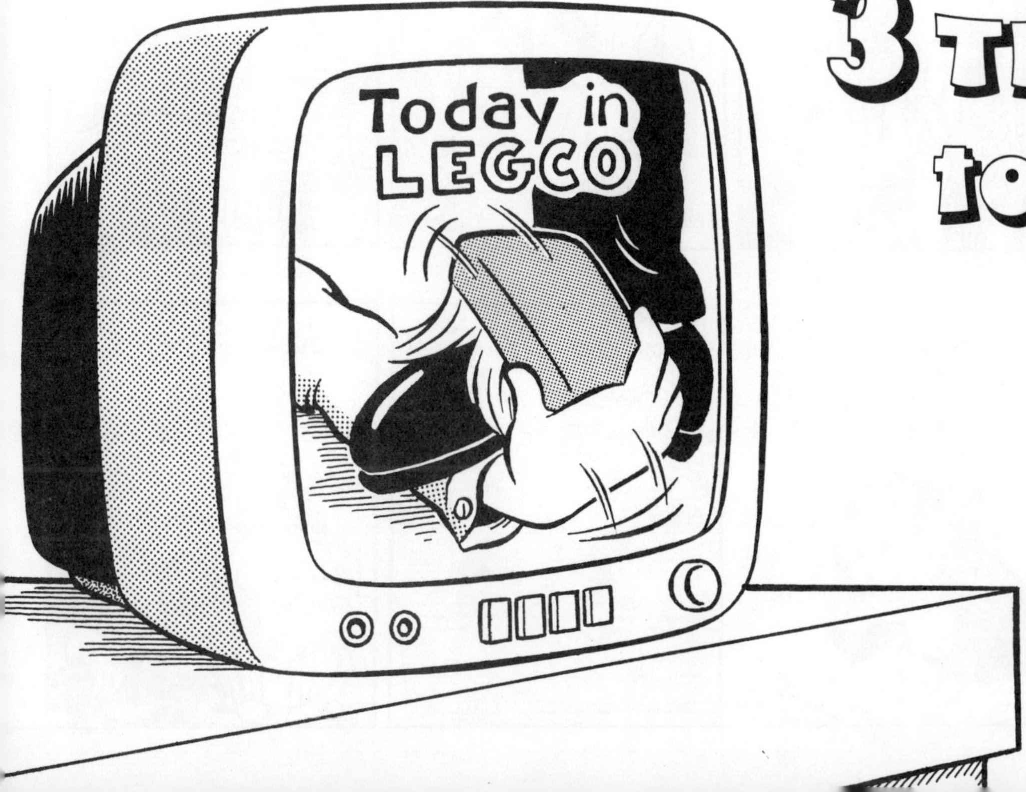
Today in
LEGCO

3 The Road to Ruin

ARE YOU WORRIED ABOUT 1997?
NO.
WHY SHOULD I WASTE MY ENERGY WORRYING ABOUT HOW THINGS WILL BE AFTER 1997?
SECOND C
ENTRAN
60¢
I NEED ALL THE ENERGY I CAN SPARE...
TIME
PLAYBOY
1997
HOT
TIME
ASIAWEEK
OUI
...JUST TO WORRY ABOUT HOW THINGS ARE NOW!
DAYA BAY
GROUP OF 81: RULE BY RICH
POLLUTION LEVELS SAFE SAYS EPD
NO TO PROVIDENT FUND
KWOK AH NUI
PRESS GAG LAW
BNO PASS-PORT
FILM CENSORSHIP
FEIGN
ALL THESE SO-CALLED "LEADERS" SHOULD KEEP THEIR MOUTHS SHUT!
MUK Tao News
GROUP OF 81 SAYS PUBLIC IS TOO STUPID TO VOTE
DENG SAYS NO TO ELECTIONS
XINHUA SAYS ELECTIONS WILL RUIN HK BEFORE WE CAN
S.Y. SAYS NO NO TO ELECTIONS
DON'T THEY REALISE? THE MORE THEY SAY, THE MORE PEOPLE LOSE CONFIDENCE AND RUSH TO LEAVE!
NEWS
BY 1997, THERE'LL BE NOBODY LEFT! THEN WHAT WILL THE BEIJING GOVERNMENT DO??
CLAIM SOVEREIGNTY OVER TORONTO?
FEIGN

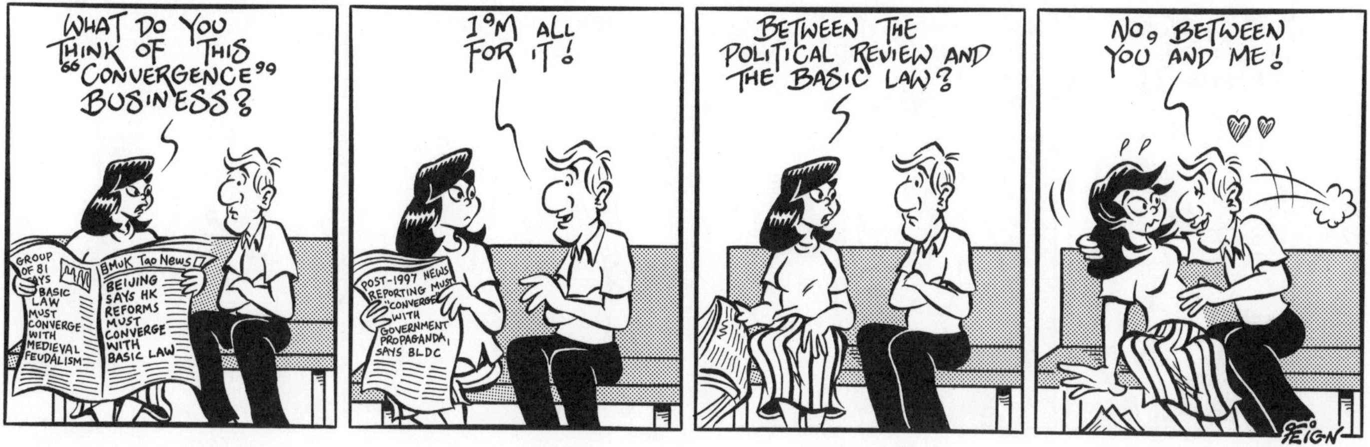
WHAT DO YOU THINK OF THIS "CONVERGENCE" BUSINESS?
GROUP OF 81 SAYS BASIC LAW MUST CONVERGE WITH MEDIEVAL FEUDALISM
MUK Tao News
BEIJING SAYS HK REFORMS MUST CONVERGE WITH BASIC LAW
I'M ALL FOR IT!
POST-1997 NEWS REPORTING MUST "CONVERGE" WITH GOVERNMENT PROPAGANDA, SAYS BLDC
BETWEEN THE POLITICAL REVIEW AND THE BASIC LAW?
NO, BETWEEN YOU AND ME!
FEIGN

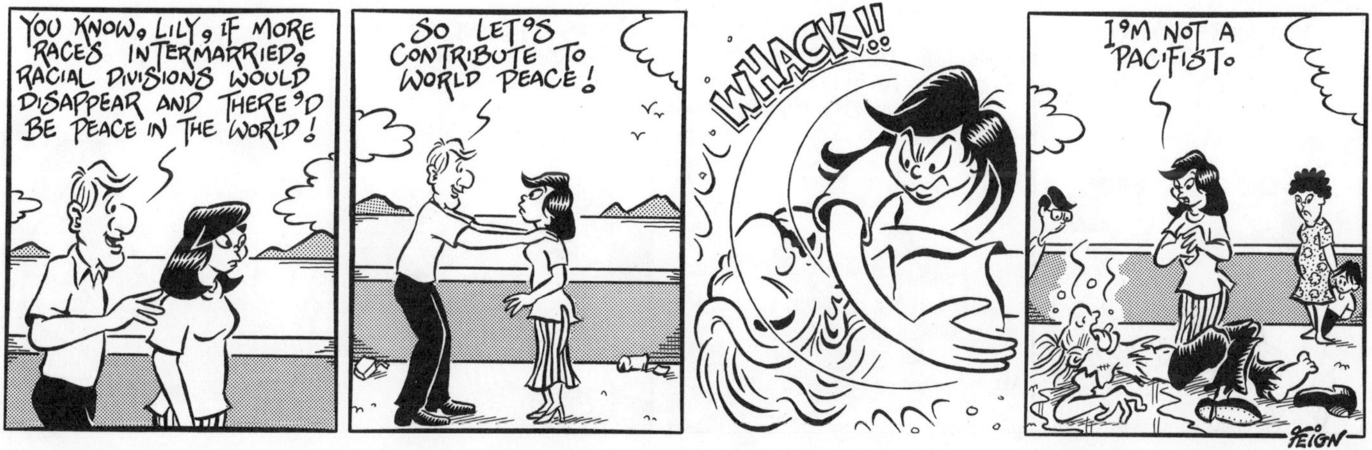
YOU KNOW, LILY, IF MORE RACES INTERMARRIED, RACIAL DIVISIONS WOULD DISAPPEAR AND THERE'D BE PEACE IN THE WORLD!
SO LET'S CONTRIBUTE TO WORLD PEACE!
WHACK!!
I'M NOT A PACIFIST.
FEIGN

QUICK, STUART! SAVE ME! GO HIDE!!
HUH? WHO IS IT? AN OLD BOYFRIEND? YOUR FATHER? YOUR BOSS?
NONE OF THOSE.
THEN HOW IS MY HIDING GOING TO SAVE YOU?
SAVE ME **MONEY**! THEY WON'T BARGAIN IF THEY SEE ME WITH A GWAILO!

YOU WERE WALKING WITH A GWAILO, WEREN'T YOU?
NO.
OH REALLY?? I'M SURE I SAW YOU WITH ONE. BIG NOSE, BROWN HAIR...
I WASN'T! AND WHAT DIFFERENCE WOULD IT MAKE IF I WAS?
ABOUT $4 A CATTY.

ONE CATTY, $8.
BUT YOU DIDN'T EVEN WEIGH IT! HOW DO I KNOW THIS IS A CATTY?
I SELL GRAPE 5 YEAR ALREADY! THIS HAND MORE ACCURATE THAN ANY SCALE!
WELL, I INSIST YOU WEIGH IT.
AHA! IT SHOWS LESS THAN A FULL CATTY!!
SEE? I TOLD YOU THIS HAND MORE ACCURATE THAN SCALE!
FEIGN

HERE'S YOUR $8.
PRICE $12!
$8
WHAT? BUT YOUR SIGN SAYS $8!
IT RAIN, SPOIL CROPS. PRICE GO UP, NOW $12.
$12
$8
BUT CROPS NEED RAIN! BESIDES, IT'S STOPPED ALREADY!
AIEEYAAA! NO MORE RAIN, BIG DROUGHT! PRICE $16!!
$16
$12
FEIGN

I'LL HAVE A CATTY, TOO.
OKAY, TWELVE DOLLAR.
WHAT?? YOU ONLY CHARGED ME $8!
$12 GWAILO PRICE!
THEN I'LL BUY IT! HERE'S YOUR $8!
LILY, YOU'RE A REAL PAL!
THAT'LL BE $12 PLEASE.
BUT A TRUE HONGKONGER AT HEART.
FEIGN

YOU REALLY BARGAINED HARD WITH THAT FRUIT HAWKER!
OF COURSE! YOU HAVE TO!!
I GUESS I'M TOO SHY TO BARGAIN.
BUT YOU HAVE TO BARGAIN FOR EVERYTHING IN HONG KONG!
OTHERWISE YOU GET RIPPED OFF!
I GUESS YOU'RE RIGHT. I'LL TRY IT FROM NOW ON.
HELLO? INLAND REVENUE? CAN WE SAY $20,000 AND CALL IT A DEAL?
INLAND REVENUE
DEMAND NOTE
$35,000
FEIGN

STUART, WE HAVE A NEW CLIENT: THE "GROUP OF 81".
MEIN KAMPF
YOU MEAN THE "RULE-BY-THE-RICH" LOBBY?
EXACTLY. THEY NEED A PUBLIC RELATIONS FIRM.
WELL, YOU CAN COUNT ME OUT! I SUPPORT DIRECT ELECTIONS!
BUT, MY DEAR STUART, SO DO THEY...
...AS LONG AS THEY'RE THE ONES WHO DIRECT THEM!
FEIGN

FIRST WE NEED A NAME FOR THE "GROUP OF 81" POLITICAL SYSTEM...
THE OTHER SIDE HAS "DEMOCRACY". WE NEED SOMETHING WITH EQUALLY STIRRING CONNOTATIONS!
"ECONOMIC AUTOCRACY"?
NO, TOO INTIMIDATING.
"NATIONALIST CAPITALISM"?
TOO WESTERN-SOUNDING. MIGHT OFFEND BEIJING.
HOW ABOUT "NATIONAL SOCIALISM"?
HMMM... NOW THAT HAS A LOVELY RING TO IT!
FEIGN

YES, CHEN, THIS SCRIPT FOR THE "GROUP OF 81" ADS ISN'T BAD...
ELECTIONS : THE ROAD TO RUIN
BUT ALL THIS TALK ABOUT DIRECT ELECTIONS BEING "DESTABILISING" AND "A RADICAL EXPERIMENT" ISN'T EXACTLY EMOTIONALLY CHARGED STUFF!
IV. RICH PEOPLE ARE GENETICALLY SUPERIOR BEINGS
IF YOU REALLY WANT TO RALLY PUBLIC SUPPORT, YOU'VE GOT TO HIT THEM RIGHT IN THE SOFT SPOT!
...AND FURTHERMORE, IF DIRECT ELECTIONS ARE INTRODUCED, HORSE RACING MAY BE BANNED...
OH MY GOD!!
FEIGN

IN THE MIDDLE AGES, FEUDAL BARONS RULED EUROPE AND MUCH OF ASIA. THINGS WERE SIMPLE THEN. IT WAS A TIME OF STABILITY AND SECURITY.
POP!
BUT, IN THE PAST 200 YEARS, AS "DEMOCRACY" HAS REARED ITS UGLY HEAD AROUND THE WORLD, WHAT HAVE WE SEEN AS THE RESULT?
BEER
TWO WORLD WARS, RIOTS, DEPRESSIONS, NUCLEAR WEAPONS, MASS STARVATION, TERRORISM, AEROPLANE CRASHES, AIDS...
LET'S GO BACK TO THE GOOD OLD DAYS... SUPPORT THE "KADOORIE PLAN" FOR RULE BY THE RICH!
URP!
FEIGN

SO, RUDY, HOW DO YOU FEEL ABOUT DIRECT ELECTIONS?
I'M AGAINST THEM.
HUH?? HOW COULD YOU BE AGAINST ELECTIONS??
EASY. LOOK WHAT HAPPENS IN OTHER COUNTRIES THAT HAVE THEM.
WHAT? SOCIAL UNREST? WELFARE HANDOUTS? HIGH TAXES?
NO, THEY BAN DRINKING ON ELECTION DAYS!
FEIGN

SIR DAVID, THERE'S GROWING PUBLIC PERCEPTION THAT THE LEGCO IS DOMINATED BY AN APPOINTED ELITE WHO DON'T TRULY REPRESENT THE PUBLIC!
AND BEIJING IS UPSET BY THE RISING DEMAND FOR DIRECT ELECTIONS! HOW CAN WE PLEASE EVERYBODY??
I'VE JUST HAD AN IDEA!
LET'S APPOINT A TOKEN "COMMON PERSON" TO LEGCO! THIS WILL ERASE THE ELITIST IMAGE AND MOLLIFY THE PRO-ELECTIONS LOBBY!
BRILLIANT! BUT WHOM DO WE CHOOSE?
PARDON ME, WAITER! I SAY, ARE YOU FREE WEDNESDAY AFTERNOONS?
FEIGN

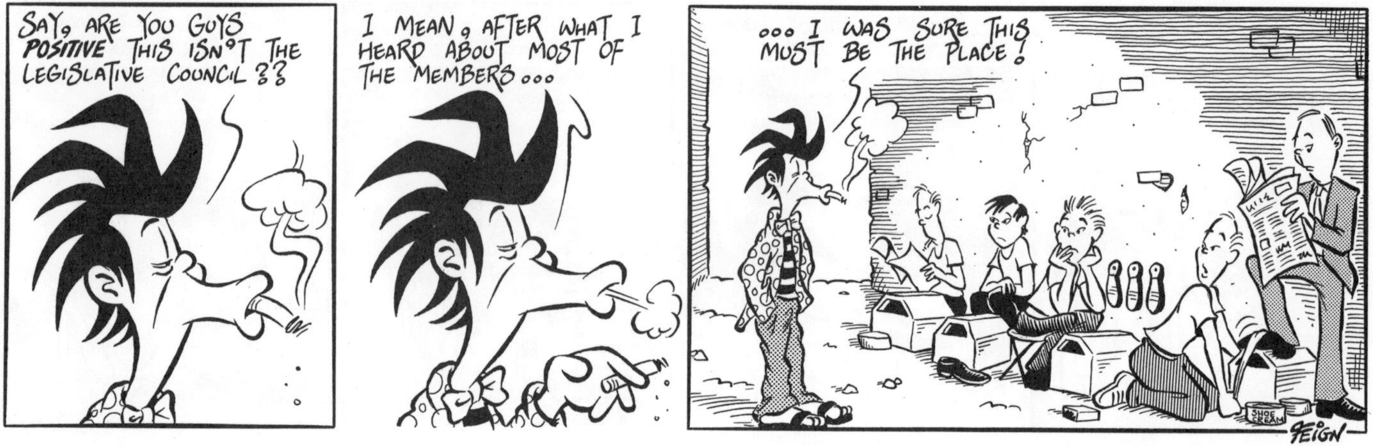
SAY, ARE YOU GUYS **POSITIVE** THIS ISN'T THE LEGISLATIVE COUNCIL??
I MEAN, AFTER WHAT I HEARD ABOUT MOST OF THE MEMBERS...
...I WAS SURE THIS MUST BE THE PLACE!
SHOE CREAM
FEIGN

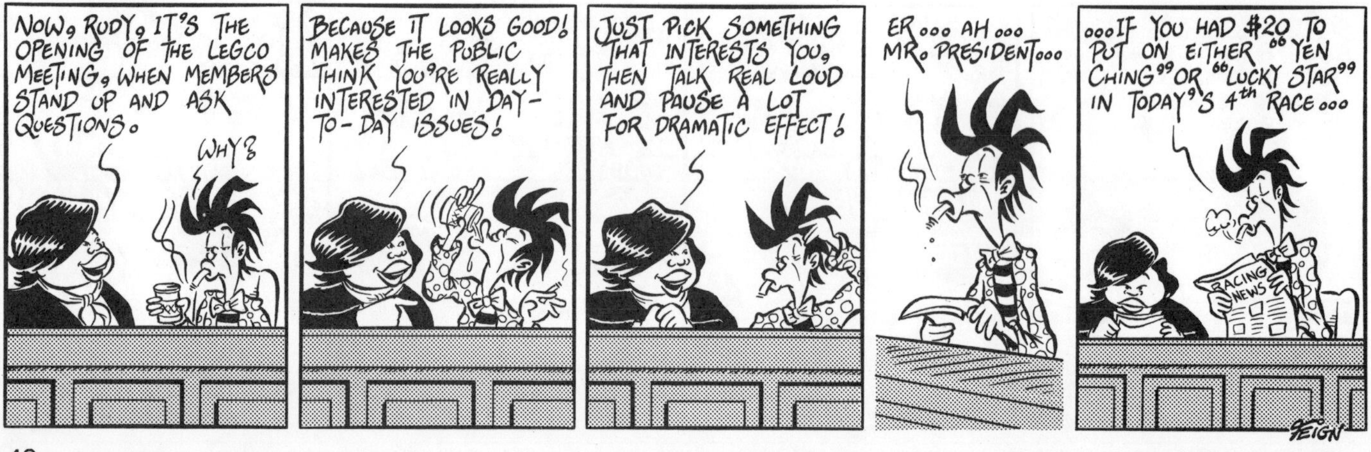
NOW, RUDY, IT'S THE OPENING OF THE LEGCO MEETING, WHEN MEMBERS STAND UP AND ASK QUESTIONS.
WHY?
BECAUSE IT LOOKS GOOD! MAKES THE PUBLIC THINK YOU'RE REALLY INTERESTED IN DAY-TO-DAY ISSUES!
JUST PICK SOMETHING THAT INTERESTS YOU, THEN TALK REAL LOUD AND PAUSE A LOT FOR DRAMATIC EFFECT!
ER... AH... MR. PRESIDENT...
...IF YOU HAD $20 TO PUT ON EITHER "YEN CHING" OR "LUCKY STAR" IN TODAY'S 4th RACE...
RACING NEWS
FEIGN

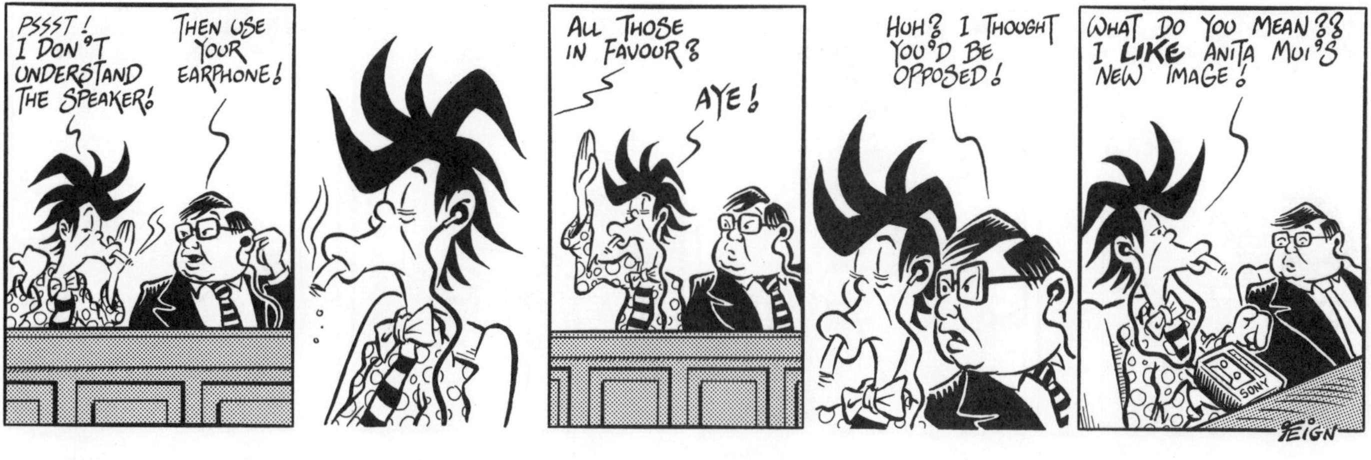
PSSST! I DON'T UNDERSTAND THE SPEAKER!
THEN USE YOUR EARPHONE!
ALL THOSE IN FAVOUR?
AYE!
HUH? I THOUGHT YOU'D BE OPPOSED!
WHAT DO YOU MEAN?? I **LIKE** ANITA MUI'S NEW IMAGE!
SONY
FEIGN

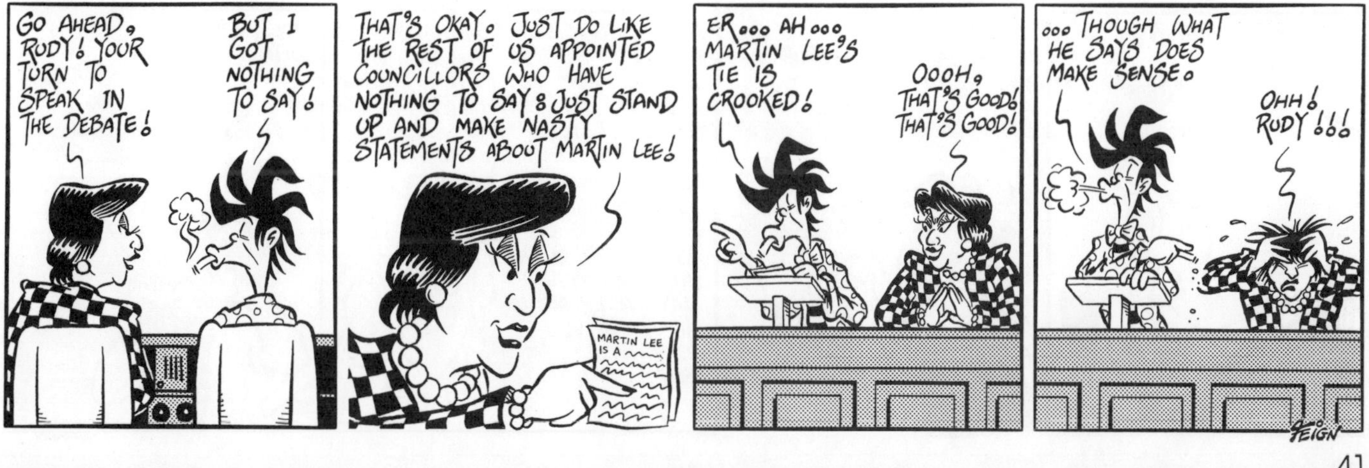
GO AHEAD, RUDY! YOUR TURN TO SPEAK IN THE DEBATE!
BUT I GOT NOTHING TO SAY!
THAT'S OKAY. JUST DO LIKE THE REST OF US APPOINTED COUNCILLORS WHO HAVE NOTHING TO SAY: JUST STAND UP AND MAKE NASTY STATEMENTS ABOUT MARTIN LEE!
MARTIN LEE IS A
ER... AH... MARTIN LEE'S TIE IS CROOKED!
OOOH, THAT'S GOOD! THAT'S GOOD!
...THOUGH WHAT HE SAYS DOES MAKE SENSE.
OHH! RUDY!!!
FEIGN

RUDY, WHY ARE YOU HOME? YOU'RE SUPPOSED TO BE AT THE LEGCO MEETING!
I QUIT! THEY LIED TO ME!
THEY TOLD ME I'D FIND THE MOST RESPECTED, IMPORTANT, INFLUENTIAL PEOPLE IN HONG KONG THERE!
BUT THEY ARE!
OH YEAH? YOU CAN'T FOOL ME!
THERE WASN'T A SINGLE FORMER MISS HONG KONG RUNNER-UP IN THE BUNCH!
CLICK!
FEIGN

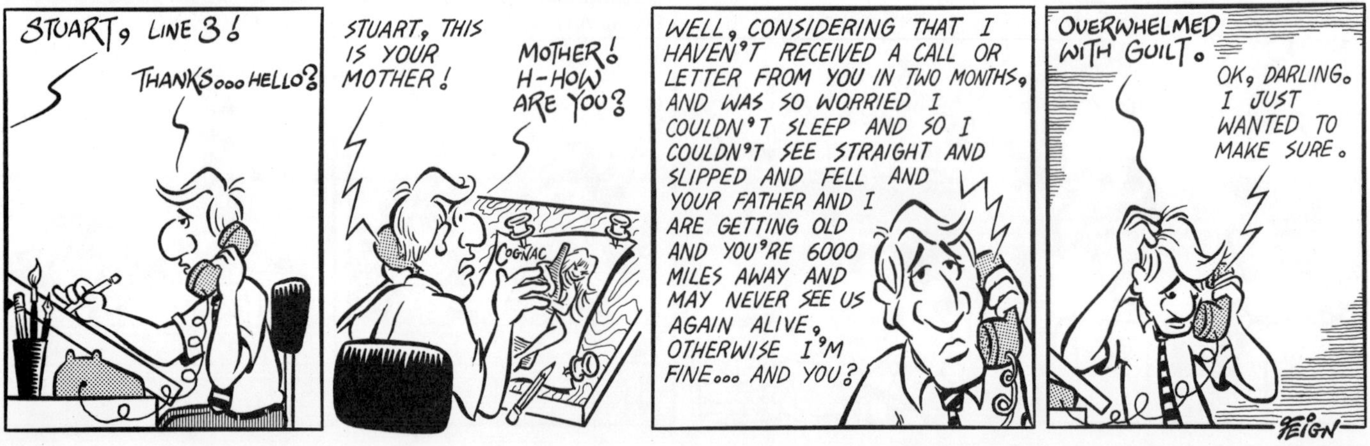
STUART, LINE 3!
THANKS... HELLO?
STUART, THIS IS YOUR MOTHER!
MOTHER! H-HOW ARE YOU?
COGNAC
WELL, CONSIDERING THAT I HAVEN'T RECEIVED A CALL OR LETTER FROM YOU IN TWO MONTHS, AND WAS SO WORRIED I COULDN'T SLEEP AND SO I COULDN'T SEE STRAIGHT AND SLIPPED AND FELL AND YOUR FATHER AND I ARE GETTING OLD AND YOU'RE 6000 MILES AWAY AND MAY NEVER SEE US AGAIN ALIVE, OTHERWISE I'M FINE... AND YOU?
OVERWHELMED WITH GUILT.
OK, DARLING. I JUST WANTED TO MAKE SURE.
FEIGN

STUART, I KNOW YOU LIKE WORKING IN THIS AD AGENCY BUT YOU'LL NEVER MAKE ANY **REAL** MONEY WITH A JOB LIKE THAT!
MEDICINE... NOW THERE'S A CAREER! JUST IMAGINE IT: **DOCTOR** STUART WR—
MR. TSY
SWEETSY
WHEEZE
MOM, FOR 26 YEARS YOU'VE TOLD ME TO BE A DOCTOR! I NEVER **WANTED** TO BE A DOCTOR! I **STILL** DON'T! ISN'T IT ABOUT TIME YOU REALISED THAT?!!
ALL RIGHT, THEN... A LAWYER.
SIGH...
FEIGN

STUART, LISTEN TO YOUR MOTHER! YOU'VE BEEN IN HONG KONG, WHAT?, TWO YEARS? ISN'T THAT ENOUGH?
ISN'T IT ABOUT TIME YOU COME HOME, SETTLE DOWN, FIND A **REAL** CAREER, **ESTABLISH** YOURSELF?
BUT, MOM, I **LIKE** IT HERE, I HAVE AN INTERESTING JOB, A DECENT SALARY, A NICE FLAT, A FEW FRIENDS... **I'M HAPPY!** WHAT MORE DO YOU WANT?
GRANDCHILDREN!!
THAT, ONE I'M WORKING ON.
FEIGN

STUART, YOU'VE BEEN ON THE PHONE WITHOUT SPEAKING FOR OVER AN HOUR!
I'M LISTENING TO MY MOTHER LECTURE ME LONG-DISTANCE!
WHAT? THERE'S NOTHING HERE BUT A DIAL TONE!
GOSH, I HOPE I SAID GOODBYE!
FEIGN

HI, SIS. THIS IS STUART. MOM TOLD ME TO CALL YOU FOR YOUR BIRTHDAY.
CLICK!
SHE SAID YOU'D GET MAD IF I DIDN'T CALL. SHE WAS REALLY NAGGING ME ABOUT IT!
I SHOULD GO WHERE ??
NO WONDER I DON'T LIKE CALLING HER!
SLAM!
FEIGN

YES, SIR, I'LL SEE IF HE'S AVAILABLE. MAY I KNOW YOUR NATIONALITY, PLEASE?
WHY, SWEDISH, BUT—
OOH! THAT'S PERFECT!! MARRIED OR SINGLE?
FAUST ASSOCIATES ADVERTISING AGENCY
HEY, I DON'T SEE WHAT—
DO YOU HAVE A CAR? ARE YOU FREE TONIGHT? HOW'S 6:30? CAN YOU PICK ME UP?
OH WELL... I WAS HOPING FOR A CANADIAN ANYWAY!
CLICK!
FEIGN

MR. McGUFF, I'D LIKE TO REQUEST A TRANSFER TO OUR TORONTO OFFICE!
I'M SORRY, I CAN'T HELP YOU, PIXIE!
SMOKE MILD DEATH
I DON'T UNDERSTAND WHY EVERYONE IN HONG KONG IS SO DESPERATE TO EMIGRATE! IT'S LIKE A MASS PANIC REACTION! TRY HAVING SOME FAITH IN THE FUTURE!
THAT'S EASY FOR YOU FOREIGNERS TO SAY! YOU CAN LEAVE ANY TIME! BUT HOW WOULD YOU FEEL IF YOU KNEW THE RUSSIANS WERE TAKING OVER AMERICA IN TEN YEARS??
I WOULDN'T GIVE A DAMN. I'M AUSTRALIAN.
SMOKE MILD DEATH
FEIGN

WHY DO YOU WANT TO MOVE TO CANADA, PIXIE?
I DON'T KNOW. EVERYBODY ELSE IS. WHY NOT ME?
YOU MEAN IT'S THAT EASY FOR YOU TO LEAVE BEHIND YOUR HOME, FAMILY AND FRIENDS?
YOU'LL BE A STRANGER IN A STRANGE LAND! A FOREIGN CULTURE! A MINORITY RACE!
HA! YOU CAN'T FOOL ME, STUART!
EVERY CANADIAN I KNOW IS CHINESE!
FEIGN

PIXIE, WHAT'S THE GOING RATE PEOPLE ARE PAYING TO MARRY SOMEONE WITH A U.S. PASSPORT?
OH, ANYWHERE FROM US$10,000 TO $20,000!
THANKS! THAT'S ALL I NEED TO KNOW!
?
HELLO, LILY? HOW'D YOU LIKE A US $10,000 TO $20,000 VALUE, ABSOLUTELY FREE...?
FEIGN

4 Darling Lily

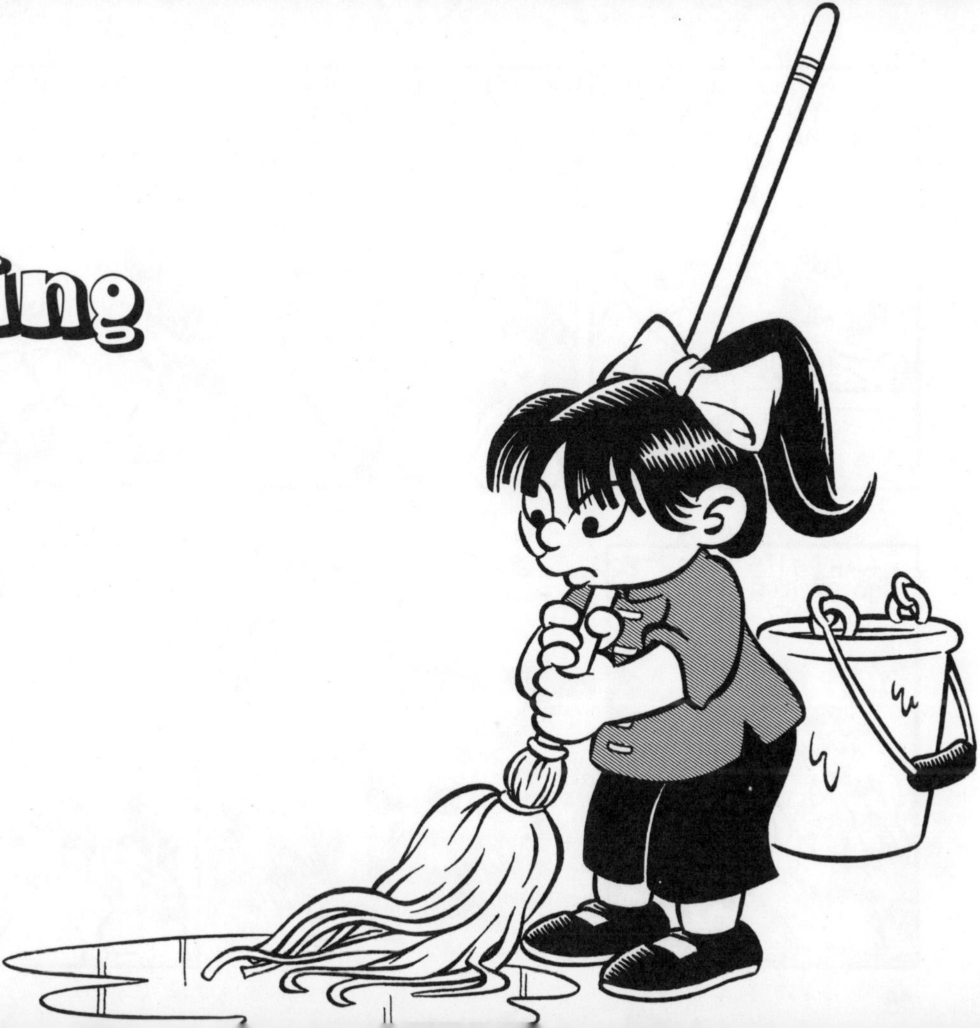

TAKE YOUR CAMERA, LILY! TODAY WE'RE GOING OUT TO MAI PO MARSHES!
REALLY, MR. NG? I DIDN'T KNOW YOU WERE A BIRD WATCHER!
BIRD WATCHER? WHAT DO YOU MEAN?
MAI PO IS A NATURE RESERVE! LOTS OF PEOPLE GO THERE TO LOOK AT BIRDS!
LOTS OF PEOPLE?
NO WONDER OUR BOARD OF DIRECTORS WANTS TO BUILD A SHOPPING MALL THERE!
FEIGN

WAH! IT'S HARD TO BELIEVE THIS IS HONG KONG!
SO QUIET AND CLEAN, NOT A BUILDING IN SIGHT!
MAI PO NATURE RESERVE
NO CROWDS, NO HAWKERS, NO RUBBISH, NO CONSTRUCTION...
...AND I SURE AS HELL PLAN TO DO SOMETHING ABOUT IT!!
MAI PO MALL
GREAT EGRET CENTRE
FEIGN

THIS BOOK IS USELESS!!
THEY LIST EVERY BIRD YOU CAN FIND...
HONG KONG BIRDS
HK BIRDS
THEY'VE GOT DETAILS OF BREEDING HABITS, SEASONAL MIGRATIONS, POPULATION DISTRIBUTIONS...
BUT WHERE THE HELL ARE THE COOKING INSTRUCTIONS??!!
FEIGN

GOOD DAY!
HELLO SIR! DO YOU COME HERE OFTEN?
EVERY CHANCE I GET!
AH! THEN YOU'LL NATURALLY WANT TO BUY SHARES IN THE MAI PO MALL, TO BE CONSTRUCTED ON THIS SITE!
SURELY YOU'RE JOKING!
NOT AT ALL! 150,000 SQUARE FEET OF PRIME OFFICE AND RETAIL SPACE, TO BE COMPLETED—
SOME PEOPLE WOULDN'T KNOW A GOOD INVESTMENT OPPORTUNITY IF IT HIT THEM ON THE HEAD!
FEIGN

WHAT'S THIS WORLD WILDLIFE FUND? SOUNDS LIKE ONE OF THOSE MANAGED UNIT TRUSTS!
WWF MAI PO VISITOR CENTRE
NO, SIR. OUR MONEY GOES TOWARD ENDANGERED SPECIES.
OH! YOU MEAN PENNY STOCKS! COULD BE LUCRATIVE!
SIR, YOU MISUNDERSTAND. WE'RE A NON-PROFIT ORGANISATION.
DID YOU SAY "NON-PROFIT"?? IN HONG KONG???
WWF MAI PO VISITOR CENTRE
WHAT ARE YOU DOING?
WAVING A $100 BILL, TO WARD OFF EVIL NON-PROFIT SPIRITS!
WWF MAI PO VISITOR
FEIGN

COME ON, LILY! WE'RE LEAVING!
BUT WHAT ABOUT THE MAI PO MALL AND GREAT EGRET CENTRE?
MAI PO NATUR RESER
FORGET IT! BAD FUNG SHUI TO BE NEAR THAT NON-PROFIT NATURE ORGANISATION. NO ONE WOULD RENT HERE.
CAN YOU IMAGINE? A NON-PROFIT ORGANISATION IN HONG KONG?! THAT'S LIKE SAYING NON-WET WATER! NON-RICH GWAILO! GIVES ME THE CREEPS!
LET'S TAKE OUR SHOPPING MALL ELSEWHERE. THIS PLACE IS FOR THE BIRDS!
I COULDN'T AGREE MORE, MR. NG...
TAXI
FEIGN

LEI LEI, IT'S TIME YOU STARTED THINKING ABOUT GETTING MARRIED.
MARQUIS DE SADE
I **HAVE** THOUGHT ABOUT IT. BUT I'M AFRAID I'LL NEVER MEET THE RIGHT MAN!
DON'T WORRY. I HAVE A FEELING YOU'LL MEET HIM VERY SOON.
OH, MA! ARE YOU SURE??
OF COURSE I'M SURE! YOUR FATHER PLACED THE AD IN THIS MORNING'S NEWSPAPER!
HUSBAND WANTED
FEIGN

WAI? YES, I ADVERTISED FOR A SON-IN-LAW. ARE YOU CHINESE?... FINE, THAT'S ALL I NEED TO KNOW.
I CAN FIT YOU IN AT 6:45 THURSDAY... OKAY? SEE YOU THEN. AND DON'T FORGET YOUR $50 FILING FEE!
$50 FEE?! WHAT ARE YOU DOING, HOLDING A RAFFLE, AND THE WINNER GETS **ME**??
CLICK!
NO, THE WINNER GETS THIS ROLEX. WHOEVER WANTS **YOU** CAN HAVE YOU!
MARQUIS DE SADE
FEIGN

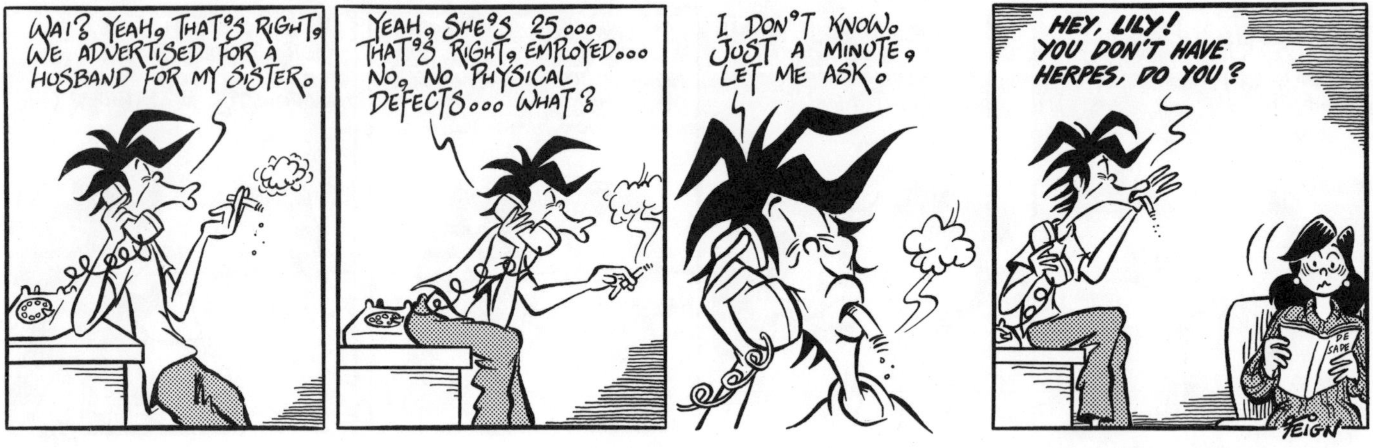
WAI? YEAH, THAT'S RIGHT, WE ADVERTISED FOR A HUSBAND FOR MY SISTER.
YEAH, SHE'S 25... THAT'S RIGHT, EMPLOYED... NO, NO PHYSICAL DEFECTS... WHAT?
I DON'T KNOW. JUST A MINUTE, LET ME ASK.
HEY, LILY! YOU DON'T HAVE HERPES, DO YOU?
DE SADE
FEIGN

LILY, MR. CHING IS HERE TO MEET YOU.
TELL ME, MR. CHING, WHAT LINE OF WORK ARE YOU IN?
YOU MIGHT CALL ME... UH ...AN INSURANCE ASSESSOR.
OH, IN OTHER WORDS, YOU DECIDE HOW MUCH TO PAY SOMEONE WHEN THEIR PROPERTY IS DAMAGED...
NOT EXACTLY...
I DECIDE HOW MUCH TO DAMAGE THEIR PROPERTY WHEN THEY DON'T PAY!
14K
FEIGN

Panel 1: MR. WONG, I WANT A WOMAN I CAN HAVE FUN WITH, WHO LIKES TO HAVE A GOOD TIME.

Panel 2: I WANT OUR RELATIONSHIP TO BE NOTHING BUT FUN AND THRILLS, PASSION AND PLEASURE!

Panel 3: MR. HO, MY DAUGHTER IS NOT LOOKING FOR A PLAYBOY, SHE'S LOOKING FOR A HUSBAND! / SO? THAT'S WHY I CAME...

Panel 4: I AM A HUSBAND!

Panel 5: WELL, DAUGHTER, HAVE YOU CHOSEN WHICH SUITOR YOU'LL MARRY? / NONE OF THEM!

Panel 6: EVERY MAN WHO'S ANSWERED THE AD HAS BEEN *NOT* ATTRACTIVE, *NOT* INTELLIGENT, *NOT* WEALTHY, AND *NOT* YOUNG!

Panel 7: "NOT THIS! NOT THAT!" WHY DON'T YOU TRY LOOKING AT THE POSITIVE SIDE?! / SUCH AS WHAT?

Panel 8: *THEY'RE NOT GWAILO!!*

HELLO, COME IN. I'M LILY. AND YOU MUST BE...
GREETINGS. I AM DR. CHIU KING FOK, ANTHONY, B.S. (H.K.) M. Sc. (Leeds), D.C.H. (Lond.), F.R.C.S. (Edin.).
ER...DO YOU MIND IF I CALL YOU BY ONLY ONE NAME?
CERTAINLY NOT! WHICH NAME DO YOU CHOOSE?
B.S.!
FEIGN

DID YOU SAY YOU'RE A DOCTOR?
A SURGEON!
Le Swanque RESTAURANT
OH! WHAT GOT YOU INTERESTED IN SLICING PEOPLE UP FOR A LIVING?
I'M FOLLOWING IN MY FATHER'S FOOTSTEPS.
WAS HE A SURGEON, TOO?
NO, A TRIAD OFFICIAL!
FEIGN

Panel 1: LILY, MARRY ME, AND I'LL GIVE YOU EVERYTHING YOU COULD POSSIBLY NEED!

Panel 2: YOU MEAN LIKE A MERCEDES, FANCY CLOTHES, DIAMONDS, VCR, SAUNA...?

Panel 3: NO, I MEAN: AN APRON, A MOP, A SPATULA, A SPONGE...

Panel 4: AND OF COURSE I'LL WANT AT LEAST 3 SONS...

Panel 5: WHAT IS THIS OBSESSION CHINESE MEN HAVE WITH PRODUCING SONS?? AS IF IT'S A *CRIME* TO HAVE ANYTHING ELSE!!

Panel 6: BUT, LILY, I NEVER INSISTED WE *ONLY* HAVE SONS...

Panel 7: IF YOU LIKE, WE CAN GET A DOG AS WELL!

IF YOU MARRY ME, LILY, I'LL LET YOU DO EVERYTHING YOU WANT!
的士
BUT I CAN DO WHATEVER I WANT RIGHT NOW! SO WHAT'S THE POINT OF MARRYING YOU??
BECAUSE UNLESS YOU MARRY ME, I CAN'T DO EVERYTHING I WANT!!
FEIGN

STUART, LET ME IN!
LILY! MY GOD! WHAT HAPPENED??
H
PANT! A MAN I WAS WITH - PANT! PANT! - TRIED TO MOLEST ME IN THE BACK OF A TAXI!... RIGHT OUT THERE!
SHOULDN'T YOU GO HOME?
NOT YET... MY PARENTS WILL NEVER UNDERSTAND!
OH? BUT WHAT IF THEY FIND OUT YOU'VE BEEN TO THE HOME OF A GWAILO?
THEN OF COURSE THEY'LL UNDERSTAND!
FEIGN

WHY DON'T YOU GET ALONG WITH YOUR PARENTS, LILY?
TO BEGIN WITH, MY FATHER ALWAYS RESENTED THE FACT THAT HIS FIRST CHILD WAS A GIRL...
IT'S A GIRL!
WHAT?!! STUPID WOMAN!! HOW DARE YOU NOT GIVE ME A SON!!
WHACK!
WHAT'S WRONG WITH HAVING A DAUGHTER?
WHAT'S WRONG?!! I JUST BET $100 ON A SON!!
FEIGN

IT WAS BAD ENOUGH BEING A GIRL, BUT THINGS GOT EVEN WORSE WHEN MY BROTHER WAS BORN...
SHUT UP NOW!! HERE COMES YOUR MOTHER BACK FROM HOSPITAL!
CLICK!
WELL?? WHAT IS IT? BOY OR UNDESIRABLE?
BOY.
A SON!! AT LAST!! MY DARLING! MY BABY! MY PRECIOUS!!
BONK
FEIGN

NATURALLY, I WAS TAUGHT THAT A GIRL'S DUTY IS TO SERVE HER BROTHER...
NOTHING'S CHANGED SINCE AGE 1...
CONGEE!
SNAP!
...AGE 7...
COKE!
SNAP!
...AND AGE 19!
CASH!
SNAP!
RACING
FEIGN

MY OWN ACHIEVEMENTS WERE BELITTLED...
STRAIGHT 100'S ON YOUR SCHOOL REPORT!
CONCEITED GIRL!! YOU MADE YOUR BROTHER LOSE FACE!!
WHACK!
... WHILE THOSE OF MY BROTHER WERE EXTOLLED...
IT WAS SIX YEARS OF HARD WORK, BUT HE MADE IT THROUGH!
SECONDARY SCHOOL?
NO, FORM 3!
FEIGN

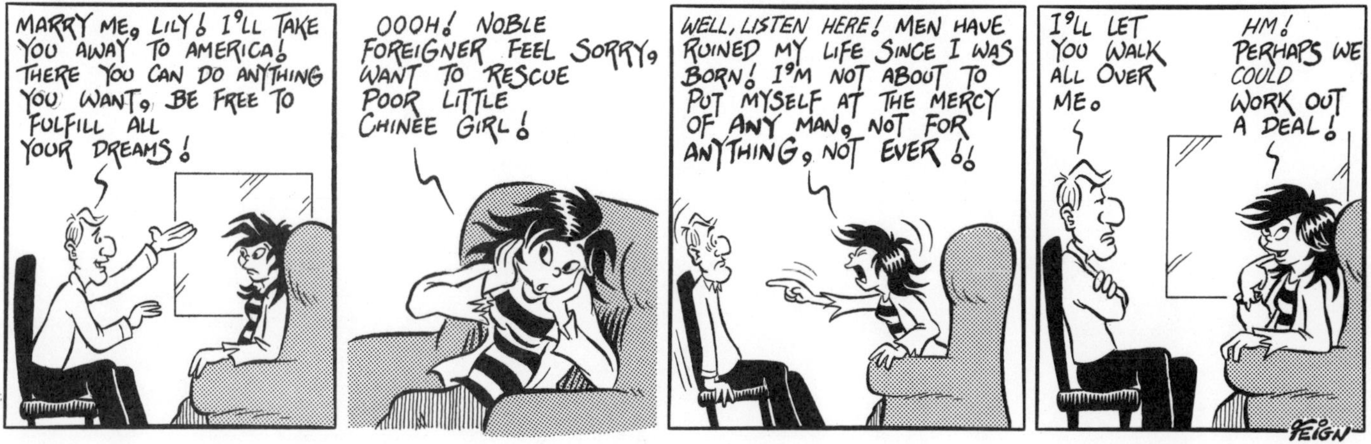
MARRY ME, LILY! I'LL TAKE YOU AWAY TO AMERICA! THERE YOU CAN DO ANYTHING YOU WANT, BE FREE TO FULFILL ALL YOUR DREAMS!
OOOH! NOBLE FOREIGNER FEEL SORRY, WANT TO RESCUE POOR LITTLE CHINEE GIRL!
WELL, LISTEN HERE! MEN HAVE RUINED MY LIFE SINCE I WAS BORN! I'M NOT ABOUT TO PUT MYSELF AT THE MERCY OF ANY MAN, NOT FOR ANYTHING, NOT EVER!!
I'LL LET YOU WALK ALL OVER ME.
HM! PERHAPS WE COULD WORK OUT A DEAL!

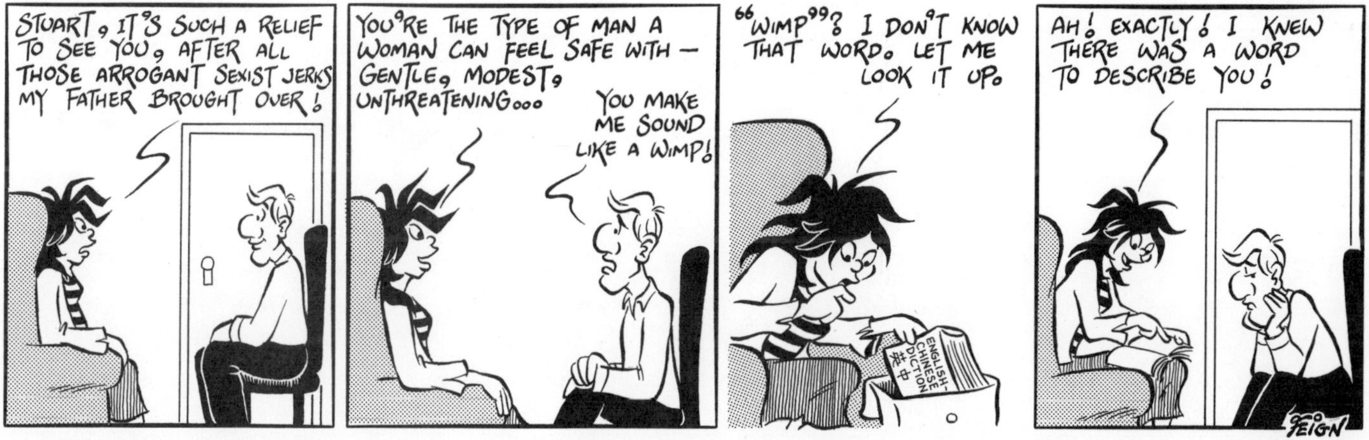
STUART, IT'S SUCH A RELIEF TO SEE YOU, AFTER ALL THOSE ARROGANT SEXIST JERKS MY FATHER BROUGHT OVER!
YOU'RE THE TYPE OF MAN A WOMAN CAN FEEL SAFE WITH — GENTLE, MODEST, UNTHREATENING...
YOU MAKE ME SOUND LIKE A WIMP!
"WIMP"? I DON'T KNOW THAT WORD. LET ME LOOK IT UP.
ENGLISH-CHINESE DICTION
英中
AH! EXACTLY! I KNEW THERE WAS A WORD TO DESCRIBE YOU!

5 Washington Bound

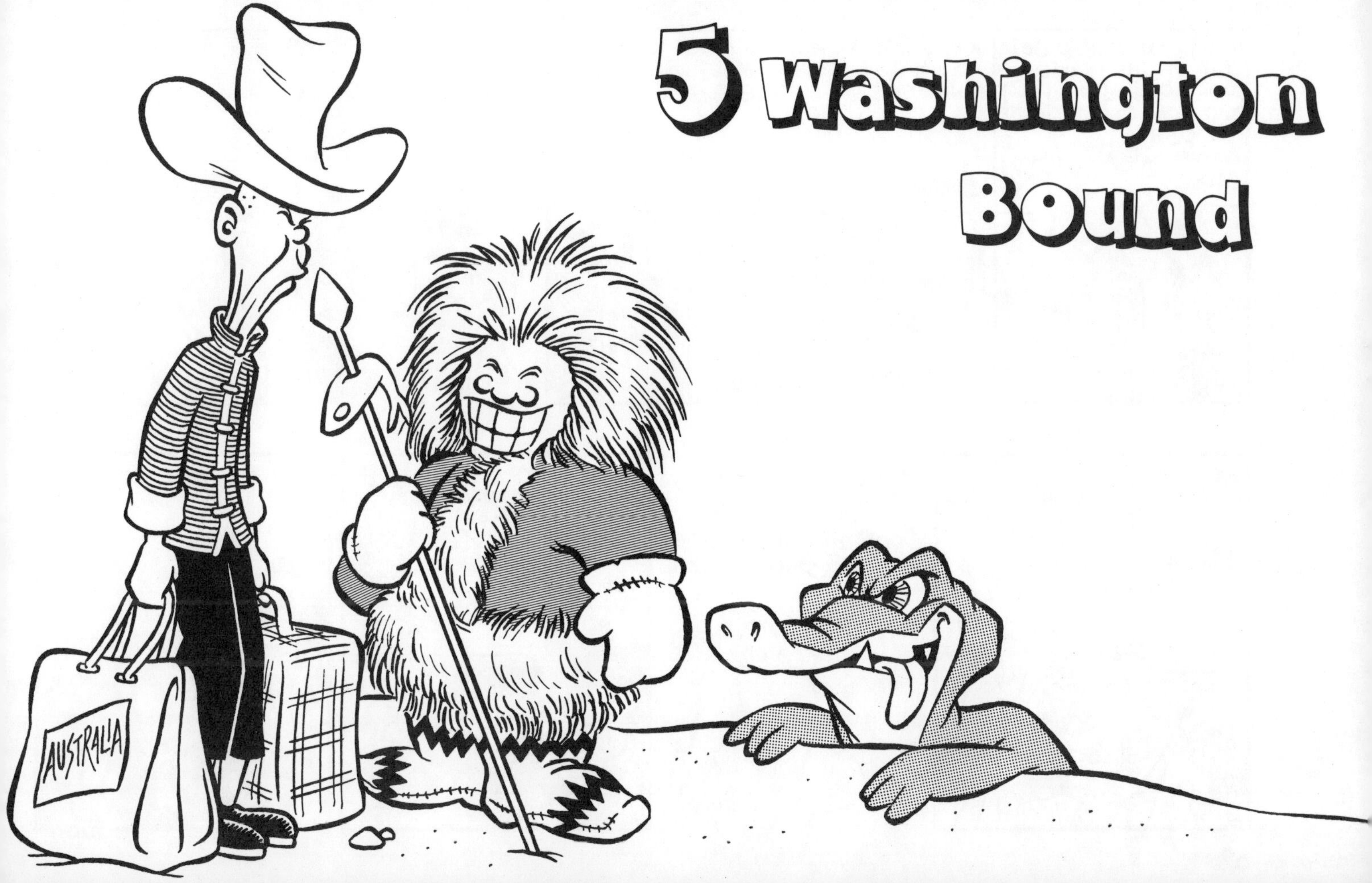
AUSTRALIA

RUDY, YOU NEED TO GET OUT OF THE HOUSE MORE OFTEN! WHY DON'T YOU JOIN ONE OF THOSE ENGLISH CONVERSATION CLUBS?
WHAT FOR?
RACING
WELL, IT'S A CHANCE TO IMPROVE YOUR ENGLISH!
SO WHAT?
MAYBE YOU'LL MEET SOME NICE GIRLS THERE!
MMMPH!
RACI
ANYWAY, YOU GOT TO PAY MONEY TO JOIN! MAY NOT BE WORTH IT.
THAT'S THE GAMBLE YOU HAVE TO TAKE!
DID YOU SAY GAMBLE??
FEIGN

WELCOME TO OUR ENGLISH CONVERSATION CLUB, RUDY! WHY DON'T YOU TELL US ABOUT YOURSELF?
I'M A WAITER.
THAT'S NICE... WHAT ELSE? WHY DON'T YOU TELL US SOME OF YOUR GOOD POINTS AND SOME OF YOUR BAD POINTS?
WELL, I SMOKE, DRINK, SPIT, JUMP QUEUES, GAMBLE, TOSS BOTTLES OUT OF WINDOWS, AND USE OUTWARD-OPENING GRILLES.
I SEE. BUT WHAT ABOUT YOUR GOOD POINTS?
THOSE ARE MY GOOD POINTS!!
FEIGN

AND HERE'S ANOTHER NEW MEMBER, MISS COOKIE CHAN! COOKIE, WHAT'S YOUR OCCUPATION?
ER... COOKIE, WHAT IS YOUR JOB?... UM... UH... MISS CHAN? I SAID, WHERE DO YOU WORK? AH... DO YOU UNDERSTAND ENGLISH...?
HELLO... MISS CHAN? ER... CAN YOU HEAR ME? ... MISS CHAN????
OH, I GET IT! YOU MUST BE A DEPARTMENT STORE SALES CLERK!
HOW DID YOU KNOW?
FEIGN

ER... WHERE ARE YOU LIVE?
NO, RUDY! WHERE DO YOU LIVE?
OH. WHERE YOU, UH... DO LIVE?
NO! VERB PRECEDES SUBJECT TO FORM A QUESTION.
SIGH! DO-YOU-LIVE-WHERE?
NO! NO! PLACE THE QUESTION WORD AT THE —
POP!
THANKS. I THOUGHT HE NEVER SHUT UP!
YEAH! WANNA GO GET A BEER?
FEIGN

YOU'RE BACK! HOW WAS THE ENGLISH CONVERSATION CLUB?
SO-SO.
OH? WELL, DID YOU MEET ANYBODY INTERESTING AT LEAST?
NO, NOBODY INTERESTING...
...BUT SHE'S REAL GOOD-LOOKING!

SO? AREN'T YOU GOING TO INTRODUCE YOUR FRIEND?
OH YEAH. THIS IS MISS CHAN.
PLEASED TO MEET YOU, MISS CHAN! I'M RUDY'S OLDER SISTER.
ER... MISS CHAN? HELLO... MISS CHAN? OH... **MISS CHAN**???
TSK! CAN'T YOU SEE SHE'S GOT HER WALKMAN ON?!
SORRY, DIDN'T MEAN TO BE RUDE.

WHO DO YOU LIKE BETTER, ALAN TAM OR LESLIE CHEUNG?
I DUNNO. HOW ABOUT YOU?
I DUNNO.
BOY! WE SURE HAVE A LOT IN COMMON!
I KNOW!
FEIGN

七月
WHAT'S THAT NOISE OUT THERE??
SHHH, AH-BA! I INVITED SOMEONE OVER FOR A DRINK.
I FINALLY GOT LUCKY, AH-BA! SHE'S WHAT I ALWAYS WANTED, WHAT I ALWAYS DREAMED ABOUT!
WHAT?!! YOU BROUGHT HOME A RACE HORSE?!!
FEIGN

RACING
RACI
WELL, I GOT TO GO.
SO SOON?? WE WERE JUST STARTING TO HIT IT OFF!
FEIGN

WHEN CAN I SEE YOU AGAIN, COOKIE?
I DON'T KNOW, RUDY. I GOT A PRETTY BUSY SCHEDULE.
I'D LIKE TO GO OUT WITH YOU, BUT I GOT MY PRIORITIES, YOU KNOW.
WOW! LIKE WHAT?
WELL, THERE'S "FIZZ BIZ" AND "ENJOY YOURSELF TONIGHT" AND "AND YET WE LIVE" AND "POLICE REPORT" AND "MACGYVER"...
FEIGN

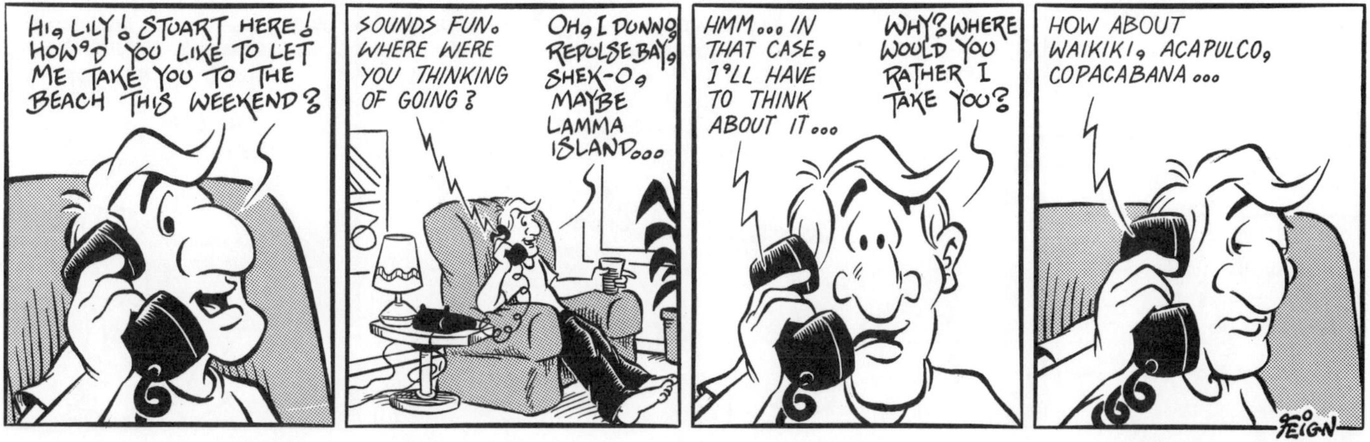
HI, LILY! STUART HERE! HOW'D YOU LIKE TO LET ME TAKE YOU TO THE BEACH THIS WEEKEND?
SOUNDS FUN. WHERE WERE YOU THINKING OF GOING?
OH, I DUNNO, REPULSE BAY, SHEK-O, MAYBE LAMMA ISLAND...
HMM... IN THAT CASE, I'LL HAVE TO THINK ABOUT IT...
WHY? WHERE WOULD YOU RATHER I TAKE YOU?
HOW ABOUT WAIKIKI, ACAPULCO, COPACABANA...
FEIGN

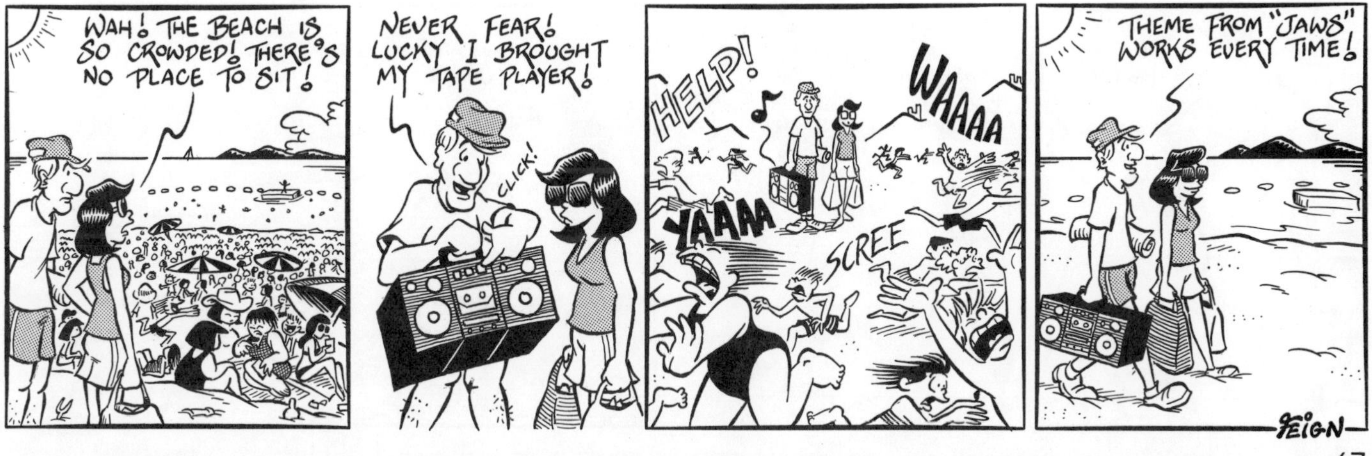
WAH! THE BEACH IS SO CROWDED! THERE'S NO PLACE TO SIT!
NEVER FEAR! LUCKY I BROUGHT MY TAPE PLAYER!
CLICK!
HELP!
WAAAAA
YAAAA
SCREE
THEME FROM "JAWS" WORKS EVERY TIME!
FEIGN

WHAT'S IN THOSE ENORMOUS BAGS?
MY BEACH SUPPLIES.
HUH? WHAT DO YOU NEED FOR THE BEACH BESIDES A SWIMSUIT AND A TOWEL?
I ♥ CATS
WELL, IN THIS BAG I'VE GOT SUN TAN OIL, LIP BALM, WATER, SNACK FOOD, TRASHY NOVEL, LOTION, INFLATABLE PILLOW, CAMERA...
AND IN THE OTHER?
PENICILLIN, DISINFECTANT, ANTIBIOTICS, HEPATITIS SERUM, CHOLERA VACCINE...
OH, I DIDN'T KNOW YOU PLANNED TO GO SWIMMING!
FEIGN

YECCH! HOW CAN ANYONE SWIM AT THIS BEACH?!!...
IT'S DISGUSTING!! I'M UP TO MY NECK IN PLASTIC BAGS, DRINK CARTONS, CIGARETTE BUTTS, HEADLESS DOLLS, AND ALL SORTS OF REFUSE, FLOTSAM AND EXCREMENT...
...AND IT LOOKS EVEN WORSE IN THE WATER!!
FEIGN

I CAN'T STAND IT! THERE'S NOWHERE TO GO TO GET AWAY FROM IT ALL ON A WEEKEND!!
THE BEACHES ARE CROWDED AND FILTHY, THE OUTER ISLAND FERRIES JAMMED, PARKS OVERRUN WITH SCREECHING RADIOS, RESTAURANTS AND SHOPPING AREAS BURSTING WITH PEOPLE...
AFTER A TOUGH WEEK AT THE OFFICE, WHERE CAN YOU GO FOR A BIT OF PEACE AND QUIET ON A SUNDAY??
THIS WAS A GREAT IDEA, LILY!
FAUST & ASS
ADVERTISING AGENCY
FEIGN

WAI! AH-YEUNG! LONG TIME NO SEE! WAH, YOU DROPPED A $100 NOTE!
$100
WHAT, ONLY $100?? HMPH! I'M SO RICH I CAN'T BE BOTHERED TO PICK UP SUCH SMALL CHANGE!
OH YEAH?? WELL, I'M SO RICH, I HATE TO SEE MY FLOOR LITTERED WITH SUCH WORTHLESS SCRAPS!
$100
SO?! SEE THIS RING? SOLID GOLD!! I DON'T NEED IT!
SEE THIS ROLEX? TOO CHEAP FOR ME!!
THEY'RE LOSING THEIR MINDS!
BETTER THAT THAN LOSE FACE!
TAILOR-MADE PANTS!
ITALIAN SHOES!!
RIP!
RRIP!
FEIGN

OUR ELDEST SON JUST ENTERED POLYTECHNIC!
OUR SON IS STUDYING ENGLISH!
OUR OTHER SON MAKES $4000 A MONTH!
HA! OUR DAUGHTER MAKES $4500!
SO WHAT?! WE'VE APPLIED TO EMIGRATE TO AUSTRALIA!!
OH YEAH?!
WELL, SO DID WE!!
WE DID?
FEIGN

SO WHY ARE YOU EMIGRATING TO AUSTRALIA?
OH, WE HAVE SO MUCH MONEY, WE CAN GO ANYWHERE...
BUT WHY AUSTRALIA ??
BECAUSE, WELL... ASK MY DAUGHTER!
LEI LEI! TELL THEM WHY WE'RE EMIGRATING TO AUSTRALIA!
WE ARE??
OF COURSE!! TELL THEM WHY!!
APPARENTLY SO YOU CAN BOAST TO THE NEIGHBOURS!
WAH! SAME REASON AS US!
FEIGN

AND I PLAN TO MARRY MY DAUGHTER OFF TO A RICH AUSTRALIAN BUSINESSMAN!
OH? WHAT'S HIS NAME?
LEI LEI! WHO'S THAT RICH AUSTRALIAN BUSINESSMAN YOU'RE MARRYING?
WINK!
WHAT RICH— OH, I GET IT! ER...ALAN BOND.
SEE? HIS NAME IS ALAN B— WHAT?!!
A GWAILO?!! I'LL KILL YOU!!!
FEIGN

SO WHICH CITY ARE YOU MOVING TO IN AUSTRALIA?
I...UH... LET'S SEE ...ER... WASHINGTON!
OH, BIG DEAL!! WE'RE MOVING TO VANCOUVER!
HA! YOU WOULDN'T CATCH ME DEAD IN VANCOUVER! TOO MANY CROCODILES!!
OH YEAH?! WELL, I HEAR WASHINGTON IS FULL OF ESKIMOS!!
SO WHAT?! PEOPLE IN VANCOUVER DON'T WEAR UNDERWEAR!!
OH YEAH?!
YEAH!!
WELL, ACTUALLY, WE'RE MOVING TO CANADA!
OH YEAH? SO ARE WE!!
FEIGN

BYE BYE! SEE YOU IN AUSTRALIA!
BYE! SEE YOU THERE!
AH-BA! HOW COULD YOU TELL THEM WE'RE MOVING TO AUSTRALIA??
BETTER THAT THAN LOSE FACE!
BUT COULDN'T YOU TELL THEY WERE JUST BOASTING?? THEY'RE NOT REALLY MOVING THERE!
THEY'RE NOT?
THEN JUST THINK HOW MUCH FACE THEY'LL LOSE IF WE DO!!
FEIGN
AIEEYAAA! LOOK AT THE CROWD!
MUST BE HALF OF HONG KONG HERE!
AUSTRALIAN CONSULATE GENERAL
HA! HA! I'LL BET THE BRITISH GOVERNMENT IS HAPPY ABOUT THIS!
ARE YOU KIDDING?? THEY'RE ANXIOUS TO DEMONSTRATE PEOPLE'S CONFIDENCE IN HONG KONG! WHY SHOULD THIS MAKE THEM HAPPY?
BECAUSE IT'S THAT MANY LESS NON-WHITES TRYING TO EMIGRATE TO THE U.K.!
FEIGN

YES, MAY I HELP YOU?
WE WANT TO EMIGRATE TO AUSTRALIA.
IMMIGRATION ·
I SEE. AND WHAT IS YOUR PURPOSE IN WISHING TO EMIGRATE?
YOU MEAN WE GOT TO HAVE A REASON?
·IMMIGRATION· ·STUDENT VISA· ·WORK PERMIT·
OF COURSE! MOST PEOPLE GO THERE INTENDING TO FIND WORK.
WORK?! WHY WOULD ANYONE GO 3000 MILES OUT OF THEIR WAY FOR THAT??
RIGHT MATE! THAT'S THE OCKER SPIRIT!
FEIGN

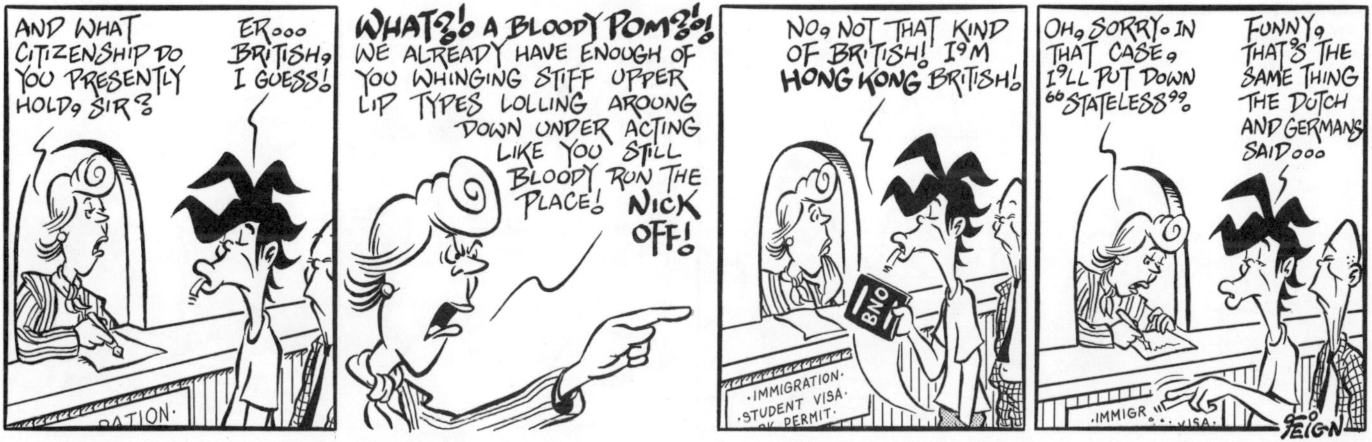
AND WHAT CITIZENSHIP DO YOU PRESENTLY HOLD, SIR?
ER... BRITISH, I GUESS!
WHAT?! A BLOODY POM?!! WE ALREADY HAVE ENOUGH OF YOU WHINGING STIFF UPPER LIP TYPES LOLLING AROONG DOWN UNDER ACTING LIKE YOU STILL BLOODY RUN THE PLACE! NICK OFF!
NO, NOT THAT KIND OF BRITISH! I'M HONG KONG BRITISH!
BNO
·IMMIGRATION· ·STUDENT VISA·
OH, SORRY. IN THAT CASE, I'LL PUT DOWN "STATELESS".
FUNNY, THAT'S THE SAME THING THE DUTCH AND GERMANS SAID...
FEIGN

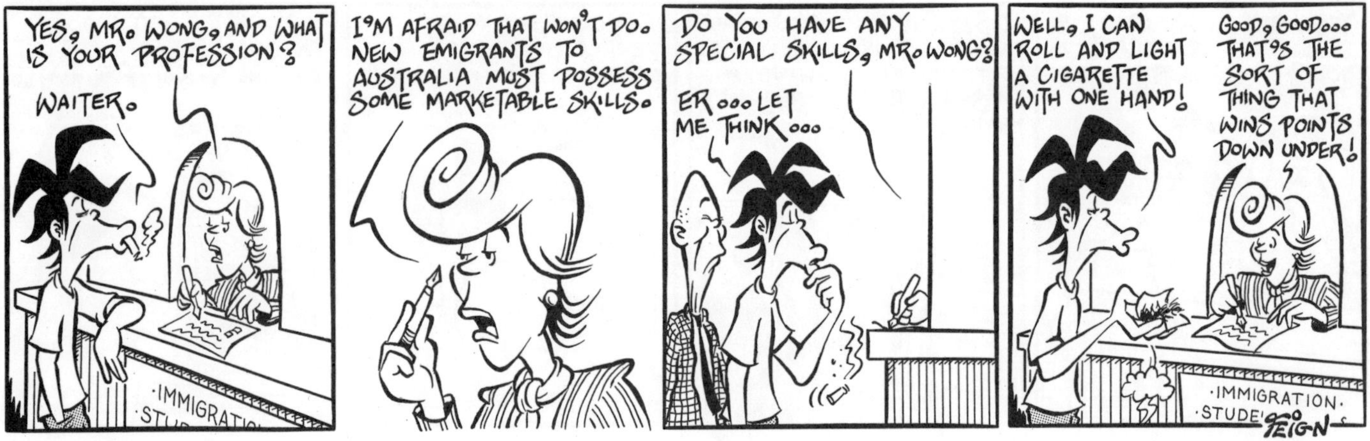

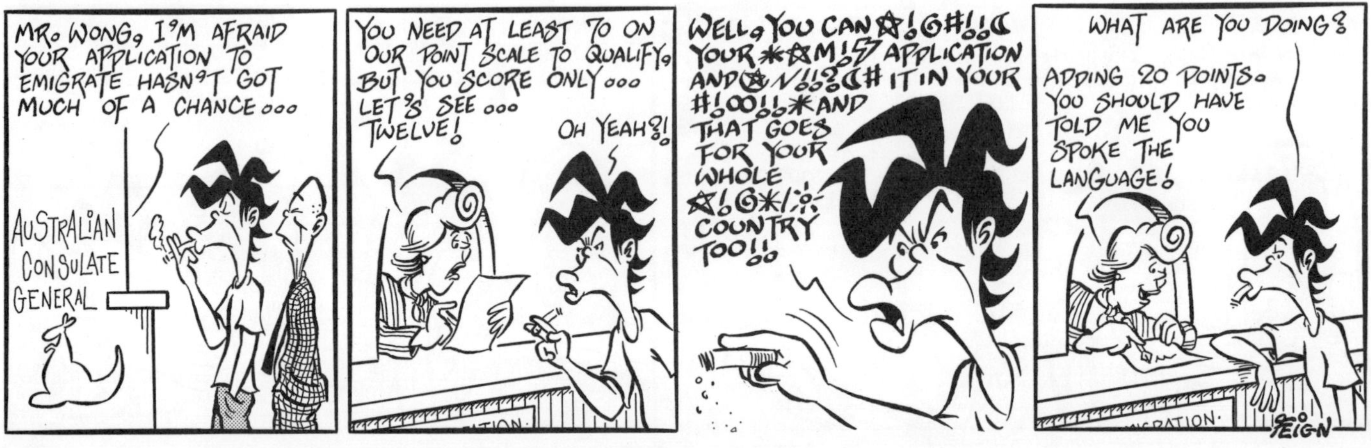

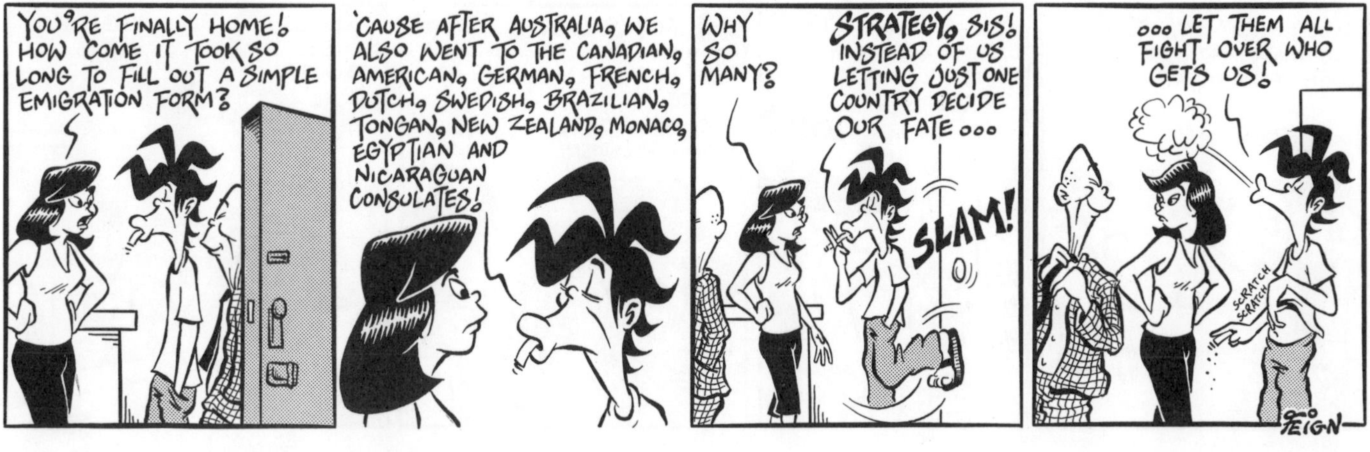
YOU'RE FINALLY HOME! HOW COME IT TOOK SO LONG TO FILL OUT A SIMPLE EMIGRATION FORM?
'CAUSE AFTER AUSTRALIA, WE ALSO WENT TO THE CANADIAN, AMERICAN, GERMAN, FRENCH, DUTCH, SWEDISH, BRAZILIAN, TONGAN, NEW ZEALAND, MONACO, EGYPTIAN AND NICARAGUAN CONSULATES!
WHY SO MANY?
STRATEGY, SIS! INSTEAD OF US LETTING JUST ONE COUNTRY DECIDE OUR FATE...
SLAM!
...LET THEM ALL FIGHT OVER WHO GETS US!
SCRATCH SCRATCH
FEIGN

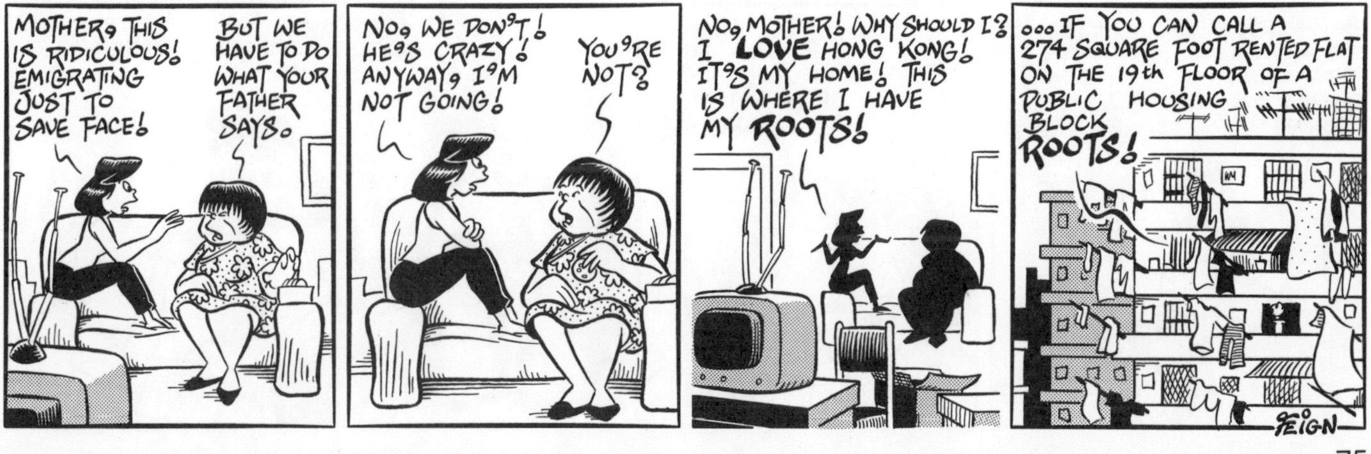
MOTHER, THIS IS RIDICULOUS! EMIGRATING JUST TO SAVE FACE!
BUT WE HAVE TO DO WHAT YOUR FATHER SAYS.
NO, WE DON'T! HE'S CRAZY! ANYWAY, I'M NOT GOING!
YOU'RE NOT?
NO, MOTHER! WHY SHOULD I? I LOVE HONG KONG! IT'S MY HOME! THIS IS WHERE I HAVE MY ROOTS!
...IF YOU CAN CALL A 274 SQUARE FOOT RENTED FLAT ON THE 19th FLOOR OF A PUBLIC HOUSING BLOCK ROOTS!
FEIGN

RUDY, WHY ARE YOU SUDDENLY SO OBSESSED WITH EMIGRATING?
AUSTRALIAN HORSE RACING
WELL, YOU KNOW THE OLD CHINESE SAYING: "THE MOON IS ROUNDER OVERSEAS".
AUSTRALIAN HORSE RACING
BUT THAT'S JUST IT! THERE'S AS MUCH CHANCE THAT THINGS ARE BETTER OVERSEAS AS THERE IS OF THE MOON REALLY BEING ROUNDER!
OH YEAH? GO LOOK!
HMM... I'M BEGINNING TO SEE YOUR POINT...
FEIGN

BAD NEWS, AH-BA! THE AUSTRALIAN CONSULATE TURNED YOU DOWN!
AH, WHO CARES!? I DIDN'T WANT TO GO THERE ANYWAY!
YOU KNOW WHAT I HEARD ABOUT THAT PLACE? THE RUBBISH COLLECTORS AND LORRY DRIVERS ARE GWAILO!
SO WHAT?
SO? IF THAT'S THE KIND OF WORK THEY GIVE GWAILO...
...JUST IMAGINE WHAT THE CHINESE HAVE TO DO!
FEIGN

6 Lily's Dilemma

BN(O)
JOBS

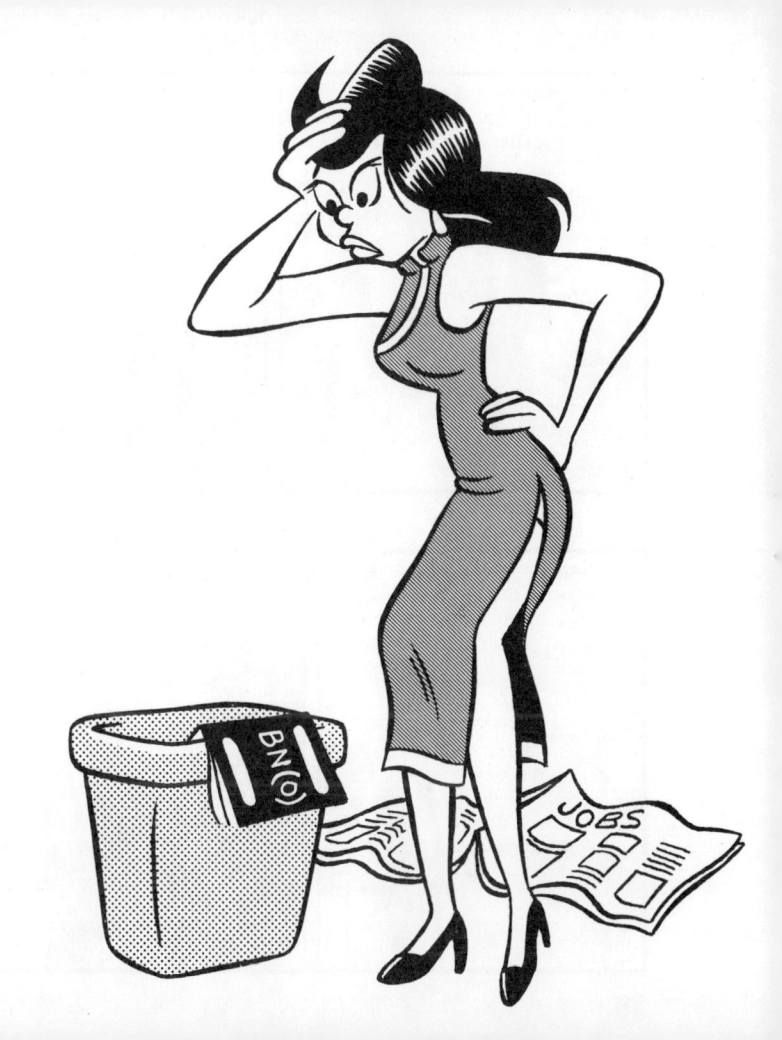

THANKS FOR COMING TO MY BOSS'S PARTY WITH ME, LILY.
TAXI
I THOUGHT YOU'D ENJOY A TYPICAL SNOOTY AFFAIR ON THE PEAK!
Ring!
AH, MR. WRIGHT! SO GOOD TO SEE YOU! DO COME IN!
AND YOUR AMAH THERE CAN WAIT IN THE KITCHEN.
FEIGN

STUART, YOUR DATE IS MAKING QUITE A HIT! SHE'S THE MOST POPULAR ONE AT THE PARTY!
HOW CAN THAT BE? WE'VE ONLY JUST ARRIVED! SHE HASN'T EVEN OPENED HER MOUTH!
SHE DOESN'T HAVE TO.
FEIGN

STUART, YOUR DATE IS LOVELY, SOPHISTICATED AND CHARMING. SHE MUST COME FROM A WELL-TO-DO FAMILY.
ACTUALLY, SHE LIVES IN A PUBLIC HOUSING ESTATE IN HUNG HOM!
I SEE. WELL, YOU MUST EXCUSE ME.
WHERE ARE YOU GOING?
TO COUNT THE SILVERWARE!
FEIGN

MISS WONG, LEST YOU THINK I'M AN ELITIST AND A RACIALIST, I WANT YOU TO MEET MY DEAR FRIEND, MRS. ALICIA HO.
$30,000 A MONTH OR LESS!
Sniff!
SEE? SHE'S EVEN WORSE THAN I AM!
FEIGN

MR. FARNSWORTH, WHY DO YOU FOREIGNERS ALWAYS EXPECT FREE HOUSING, CARS, CLUB FEES, PLANE FARE, INSURANCE, AND SO ON, ON TOP OF YOUR ENORMOUS SALARIES?
IT'S ONLY NATURAL, MISS WONG. AFTER ALL, HONG KONG IS CONSIDERED A HARDSHIP POST.
YOU CALL THIS **HARDSHIP**?! YOU EXPATS LIVE LIKE **KINGS AND QUEENS** WHILE THE AVERAGE LOCAL EARNS LESS IN A MONTH THAN YOU'LL SPEND FOR A NIGHT OUT!!
I DIDN'T SAY IT WAS HARDSHIP FOR **US**!!
FEIGN

ISN'T IT UNFAIR THAT YOU FOREIGNERS, ALREADY HIGHLY PAID, ALSO GET FREE HOUSING, PAID TRAVEL, CARS, MAIDS, INSURANCE, AND OTHER PERKS?
NOT AT ALL! WE'VE LEFT OUR HOMES BEHIND TO COME HERE TO WORK. IT'S ONLY NATURAL THAT OUR NEEDS BE TAKEN CARE OF.
OH? THEN HOW COULD I EXPECT TO BE TREATED IF I WENT TO YOUR COUNTRY TO WORK?
WHY, AS ANOTHER UNWELCOME ASIAN IMMIGRANT, OF COURSE!
FEIGN

YOU KNOW, COOKIE, IF YOU REALLY LOVE ME, YOU'LL... Whisper... Bzz bzz bzz...
LUI FONG FAN CLUB NEWS
WHAT?! NO WAY, RUDY! THAT COULD BE FATAL!
AW, C'MON! YOU DON'T BELIEVE ALL THAT RUBBISH ABOUT AIDS, DO YOU?
I'M NOT TALKING ABOUT AIDS...
... I'M TALKING ABOUT MY FATHER!
FEIGN

COOKIE, THERE'S NO WAY ME OR ANYONE IN MY FAMILY COULD HAVE AIDS!
LUI FONG FAN CLUB NEWS
OH YEAH? YOU SAID YOUR SISTER HAS A GWAILO BOYFRIEND. BY NOW SHE MUST HAVE AIDS!
LUI
NO WAY! THE ONLY PHYSICAL THING SHE'S EVER DONE WITH HIM IS SLAP HIS FACE!
AHA! BUT DID HE BLEED ON HER?
HMM... YOU GOT A POINT...!
FEIGN

ISN'T THERE A WAY TO PREVENT AIDS?
YEAH, THERE IS. IT'S SOMETHING THEY CALL A CONDOM.
WHAT'S THAT?
I DUNNO. SOMETHING I HEARD ABOUT ON TV.
I THINK IT HAS SOMETHING TO DO WITH PYRAMIDS!
WAH! IT MUST HURT!
FEIGN

ARE YOU SURE AIDS ONLY AFFECTS FOREIGNERS?
OF COURSE I'M SURE! HOW MANY CHINESE DO YOU KNOW WHO HAVE AIDS?
NONE.
RIGHT. AND HOW MANY FOREIGNERS DO YOU KNOW WHO DON'T HAVE AIDS?
I DON'T KNOW ANY FOREIGNERS.
SEE? THAT PROVES MY POINT!
WAH! SCARY, ISN'T IT?
FEIGN

SIGH... I DON'T THINK WE SHOULD DO IT, RUDY.
I MEAN, WITH AIDS AND HERPES AND EVERYTHING, IT'S JUST TOO SCARY!
YOU'RE RIGHT. WE SHOULDN'T GAMBLE.
AIEEYAAA! WHAT DID I JUST SAY??
THERE, THERE. I WASN'T EVEN LISTENING.
FEIGN

I'M HUNGRY. LET'S GO EAT AT ONE OF THOSE LITTLE BACK-STREET RESTAURANTS.
THOSE LITTLE PLACES USUALLY USE A LOT OF MSG. AREN'T YOU CONCERNED ABOUT THAT?
NOT REALLY.
WHEN I EAT OUT IN HONG KONG...
...MSG IS THE LEAST OF MY WORRIES!
RADIOACTIVE OYSTERS
HEPATITIS EPIDE
POISON CHOI SU
SCMP
STEROIDS IN POULTRY
POLLUTED SHELLFISH
FEIGN

WHAT SHALL WE ORDER? DO YOU WANT CHICKEN?
NO WAY!! THEY'RE PUMPED FULL OF TOXIC GROWTH HORMONES!
牌菜 MENU
HOW ABOUT FISH?
CLAMS?
NO, FULL OF CYANIDE!
WE'LL CATCH HEPATITIS!
VEGETABLES?
PORK?
OYSTERS?
INFUSED WITH PESTICIDES!
STEROIDS!!
CADMIUM, LEAD, COPPER...
牌菜 MENU
GOLDEN DUCK
THEN PERHAPS A DRINK. WINE?
BEER?
OKAY, PLAIN BOTTLED WATER.
ANTI-FREEZE!
ADDITIVES!!
PROBABLY UNFILTERED TAP WATER!
WHAT'LL IT BE, SIR?
TWO NAPKINS AND A SIDE ORDER OF TOOTHPICKS.
FEIGN

LOOK AT THAT! THEY NET THE POOR FISH RIGHT IN FRONT OF YOU!
I CAN'T BEAR TO WATCH!
DON'T WORRY, THEY DON'T NET THEM HERE. THEY USE TRADITIONAL HONG KONG FISHING METHODS...
DYNAMITE AND CYANIDE.
KABOOSH
POISON
FEIGN

TSK! FLIES ARE GETTING ALL OVER THE VEGETABLES!
WAITER! CAN'T YOU GET RID OF ALL THE FLIES IN HERE?!
NO NEED.
WHY NOT?
THE DDT ALREADY DID.
FEIGN

THAT PORK YOU'RE EATING WAS INJECTED WITH HORMONES AND ANTIBIOTICS...
...CAGED AND SLAUGHTERED IN INHUMANE CONDITIONS, ITS EXCREMENT FOULING OUR WATERS, STORED AND COOKED IN UNSANITARY FACILITIES...
BESIDES, PIGS ARE SENTIENT BEINGS, TOO, YOU KNOW! THEY'RE SMARTER THAN DOGS! THEY'RE —
WHOMP!
...RATHER TASTY, AREN'T THEY?
FEIGN

CARE FOR ANYTHING ELSE?
WHAT WOULD YOU RECOMMEND?
A LARGE TIP AND A HASTY EXIT!
FEIGN

I FEEL ILL. I NEED TO SEE THE DOCTOR.
DOCTOR IS OUT. YOU COME BACK LATER.
POP STARS
LATER...
OOG... IS THE DOCTOR IN YET?
STILL NOT HERE. YOU COME BACK LATER.
STILL LATER...
THE DOCTOR'S STILL NOT IN?? ARRGGH... WHEN WILL HE RETURN?
AS SOON AS HE GETS LANDED IMMIGRANT STATUS IN CANADA.
FEIGN

WRIGHT, WHAT'S WRONG?
I FEEL SICK. MY DOCTOR'S OUT OF TOWN. I ~~~
QUICK! GET HIM TO A HOSPITAL!
THNUMP
HELP! OUR FRIEND NEEDS MEDICAL ATTENTION!
SORRY, SIR. WE HAVE A SHORTAGE OF DOCTORS.
Hong Kong Government Hospital
OUTPATIENT REGISTRATION
...BUT OUR MIDWIFE WON'T BE EMIGRATING TILL THIS AFTERNOON. I SUPPOSE SHE COULD FIT YOU IN.
FEIGN

I DON'T BELIEVE IT! STUART COULD BE DYING AND WE CAN'T FIND HELP!
OUTPATIENT CLINIC
HIS OWN PHYSICIAN EMIGRATED, THERE'S NO ONE TO HELP IN THE HOSPITALS BECAUSE OF THE SHORTAGE OF MEDICAL PROFESSIONALS...
WHERE THE HELL CAN YOU GO TO FIND A DOCTOR IN THIS TOWN?!
TAXI
Kai Tak International Airport DEPARTURES
TAXI
MK2137
FEIGN

DEPARTING FLIGH
EXCUSE ME. OUR COLLEAGUE IS SICK. ARE YOU A DOCTOR?
PASSENGERS ONLY BEYOND THIS POINT
NO, I'M AN ACCOUNTANT.
PARDON ME, IS ANY OF YOU A DOCTOR?
COMPUTER PROGRAMMER.
NO, CURRENCY BROKER.
TV STAR.
HELLO, I'M A DOCTOR.
YES.
AND YOU'RE EMIGRATING TO CANADA?
11.57
12.10
MARRIED OR SINGLE?
FEIGN

YOUR FRIEND IS EXPERIENCING GASTROINTESTINAL PAIN BROUGHT ON BY MILD FOOD POISONING. I'LL GIVE HIM THIS ANTACID.
I'D PRESCRIBE A PAINKILLER, BUT I'M AFRAID I DON'T HAVE MY FORMS.
OH, THAT'S NO PROBLEM.
ATTENTION! IS THERE AN INTERNATIONAL DRUGS COURIER IN THE HOUSE?
COKE?
SMACK?
PCP?
THIS IS KAI TAK AIRPORT, AFTER ALL.
FEIGN

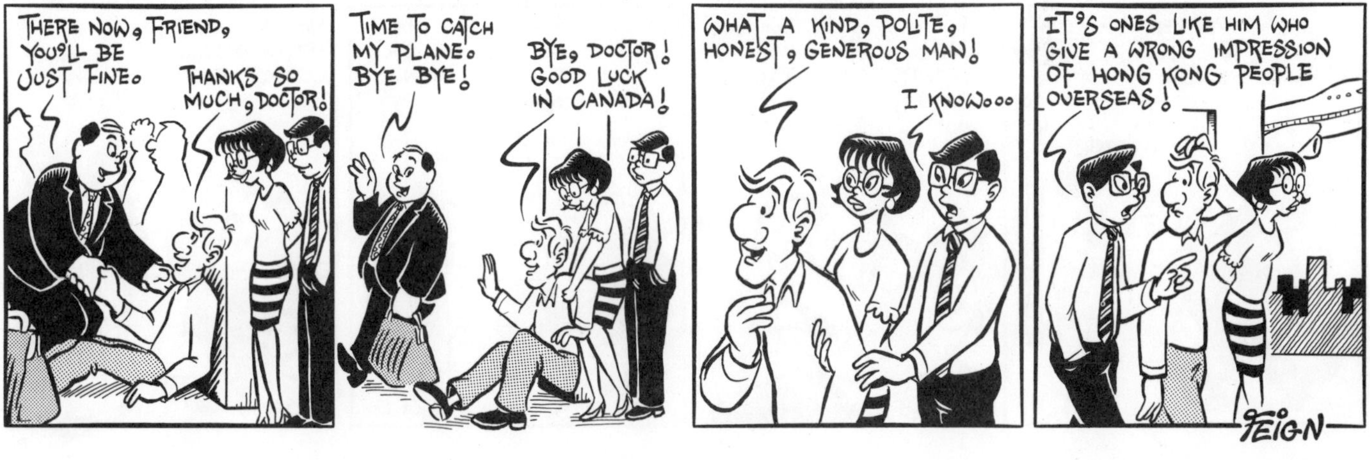
THERE NOW, FRIEND, YOU'LL BE JUST FINE.
THANKS SO MUCH, DOCTOR!
TIME TO CATCH MY PLANE. BYE BYE!
BYE, DOCTOR! GOOD LUCK IN CANADA!
WHAT A KIND, POLITE, HONEST, GENEROUS MAN!
I KNOW...
IT'S ONES LIKE HIM WHO GIVE A WRONG IMPRESSION OF HONG KONG PEOPLE OVERSEAS!
FEIGN

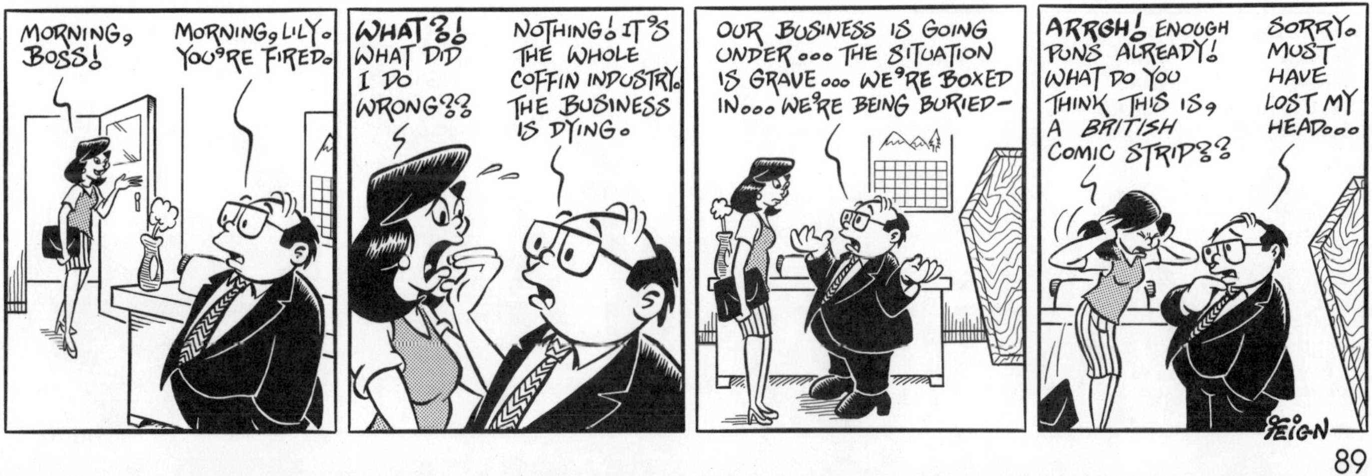
MORNING, BOSS!
MORNING, LILY. YOU'RE FIRED.
WHAT?! WHAT DID I DO WRONG??
NOTHING! IT'S THE WHOLE COFFIN INDUSTRY. THE BUSINESS IS DYING.
OUR BUSINESS IS GOING UNDER ... THE SITUATION IS GRAVE ... WE'RE BOXED IN... WE'RE BEING BURIED—
ARRGH! ENOUGH PUNS ALREADY! WHAT DO YOU THINK THIS IS, A BRITISH COMIC STRIP??
SORRY. MUST HAVE LOST MY HEAD...
FEIGN

LILY, I'VE DECIDED TO QUIT THE COFFIN BUSINESS.
BUT WHY? IT'S BEEN DOING SO WELL!
FOR NOW, MAYBE. BUT LOOK AT THE LONG-TERM TRENDS! WE'LL PROBABLY BE OUT OF BUSINESS BY 1997!
WHY? YOU THINK NO ONE WILL BE DYING IN HONG KONG AFTER 1997?
NO, I THINK NO ONE WILL BE *LIVING* IN HONG KONG AFTER 1997!
FEIGN

WHAT WILL YOU DO AFTER YOU SELL THE BUSINESS?
TAKE THE MONEY AND MOVE TO AUSTRALIA.
AUSTRALIA? WHY THERE?
I WANTED AN ENGLISH-SPEAKING COUNTRY WHERE THE ECONOMY IS HEALTHY, THE FOOD IS GOOD, THE PEOPLE ARE OPEN-MINDED...
BUT LACKING THOSE, I'LL SETTLE FOR AUSTRALIA.
FEIGN

LILY, IN GRATITUDE FOR YOUR SEVEN YEARS OF LOYAL AND DEVOTED SERVICE, I'D LIKE TO PRESENT YOU WITH THIS GENUINE GOLD ROLEX WATCH!
WHY, MR. NG! HOW THOUGHTFUL! I'M DEEPLY TOUCHED.
OF COURSE, THAT'S IN LIEU OF YOUR LAST MONTH'S SALARY...
WHACK
LILY, I'M DEEPLY TOUCHED... IN FACT, **TOO** DEEPLY...!
FEIGN

I DON'T BELIEVE IT! **ME**, FIRED FROM MY JOB!
HAPPY LUCKY
GOLDEN FORTUNE
BRIGHTER SUCCE
CO. LTD.
SLAM!
GRRR! I'M SO *HUMILIATED*, SO **MAD**! IF ANYONE SAYS A WORD, I'LL... I'LL...
EXCUSE ME, MISS, COULD YOU PLEASE TELL ME —
HK MAP
WHOOSH
WHAM!
JEEZ! I'M USED TO RUDE TREATMENT IN HONG KONG, BUT WHERE DO YOU THINK YOU ARE, LADY... *NEW YORK*??
Aaah...
FEIGN

I CAN'T JUST SIT HERE FEELING SORRY FOR MYSELF OVER LOSING MY JOB...
I KNOW! I'LL CHEER MYSELF UP BY HAVING A CUP OF TEA, A CAKE, AND READING THE PAPER!
HongKong STANDARD
12 INJURED IN KOWLOON BUS CRASH
TERRORISM
ACTOR DEAD AT 67
AIDS PANIC
HK MAN EXECUTED IN CHINA FOR JAYWALKING
HongKong Standard
GULF WAR
200 DEAD IN DELHI RIOTS
MASS MURDER IN L.A.
COUP IN MANILA
SUICIDE
CHINA EARTHQUAKE
IT WAS SIMPLER FEELING SORRY JUST FOR MYSELF!
FEIGN

HMM... HERE'S A DECENT JOB: "EXECUTIVE SECRETARY, MULTINATIONAL BANK, FEMALE, FLUENT ENGLISH A MUST."
RIP!
JOBMARKET
MUST BE WORKING FOR A GWAILO. WELL, MIGHT AS WELL GIVE IT A TRY!
EXECUTIVE SECRETARY
BUT I'VE NEVER WORKED FOR A FOREIGNER! HOW DO I PRESENT MYSELF? WHAT ARE MOST FOREIGN MEN LOOKING FOR IN A SECRETARY?
TB TOWN BANK
Personnel Dept.
FEIGN

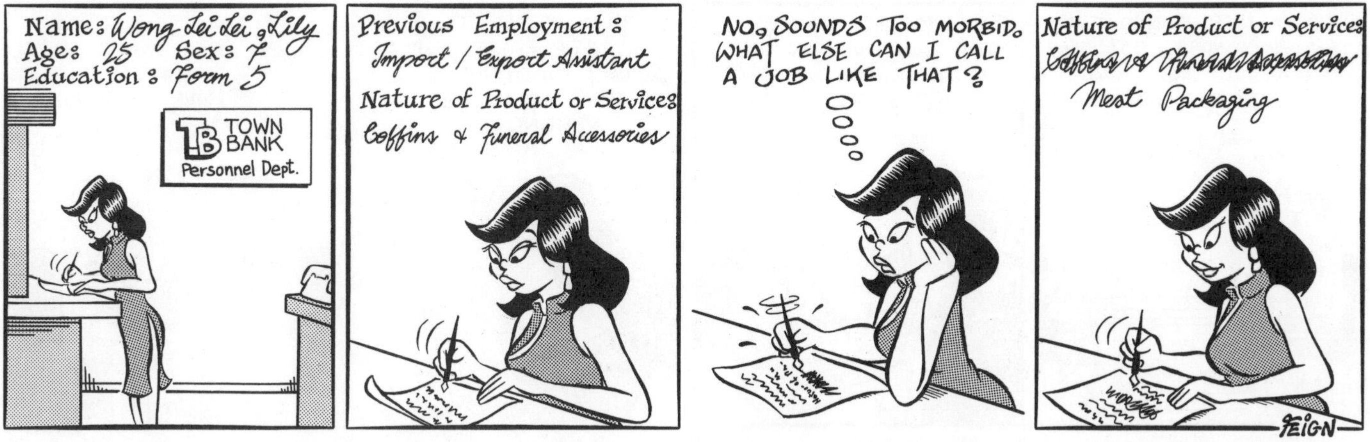
Name: Wong Lei Lei, Lily
Age: 25 Sex: F
Education: Form 5
TB TOWN BANK Personnel Dept.
Previous Employment:
Import / Export Assistant
Nature of Product or Services:
Coffins & Funeral Accessories
NO, SOUNDS TOO MORBID. WHAT ELSE CAN I CALL A JOB LIKE THAT?
Nature of Product or Services:
Meat Packaging
FEIGN

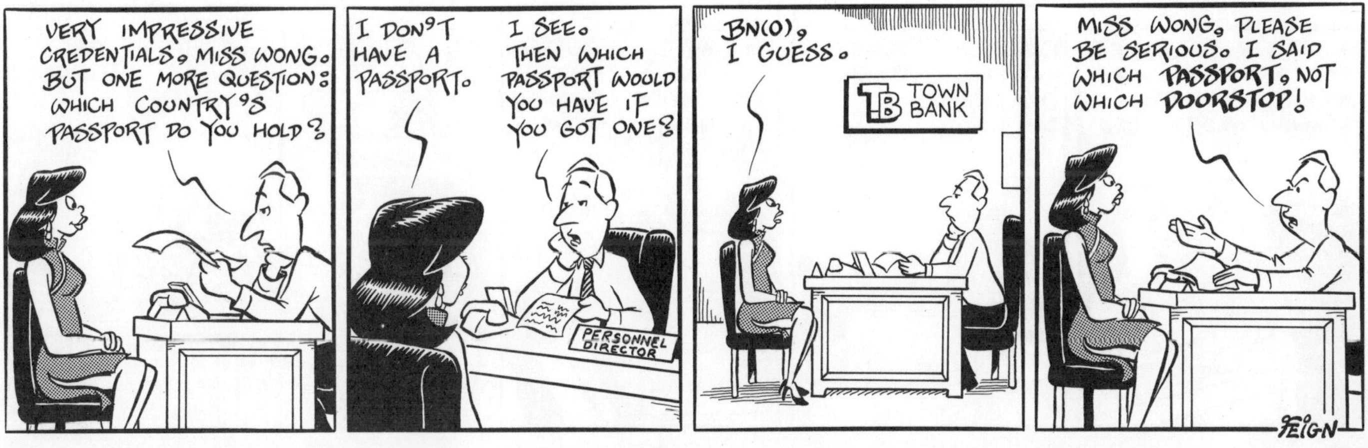
VERY IMPRESSIVE CREDENTIALS, MISS WONG. BUT ONE MORE QUESTION: WHICH COUNTRY'S PASSPORT DO YOU HOLD?
I DON'T HAVE A PASSPORT.
I SEE. THEN WHICH PASSPORT WOULD YOU HAVE IF YOU GOT ONE?
PERSONNEL DIRECTOR
BN(O), I GUESS.
TB TOWN BANK
MISS WONG, PLEASE BE SERIOUS. I SAID WHICH PASSPORT, NOT WHICH DOORSTOP!
FEIGN

YOU'RE WELL-SUITED FOR THE JOB, MISS. BUT I'M AFRAID WE ONLY HIRE LOCAL PEOPLE WHO HAVE FOREIGN PASSPORTS.
WHY?
BECAUSE THE OTHERS KEEP QUITTING ON US TO EMIGRATE. WE CAN'T AFFORD SUCH TURNOVER.
PERSONNEL DIRECTOR
BUT WHAT ABOUT PEOPLE LIKE **ME**, WHO DON'T **WANT** TO LEAVE? DON'T YOU HAVE CONFIDENCE IN HONG KONG???
OF COURSE WE DO! WE JUST DON'T HAVE CONFIDENCE IN PEOPLE WHO HAVE CONFIDENCE IN HONG KONG.
FEIGN

MISS WONG, YOU'RE RIGHT FOR THE JOB, BUT I'M AFRAID WE ONLY HIRE PEOPLE WITH FOREIGN PASSPORTS.
PERSONNEL DIRECTOR
BUT I REALLY WANT THE JOB! WHAT CAN I DO?
GET A FOREIGN PASSPORT.
OH, COME ON! HOW AM I SUPPOSED TO GET FOREIGN CITIZENSHIP OVERNIGHT??
YOU COULD MARRY A FOREIGN NATIONAL.
CAN YOU HOLD THE JOB TILL MONDAY?
OKAY, BUT NO LONGER!
FEIGN

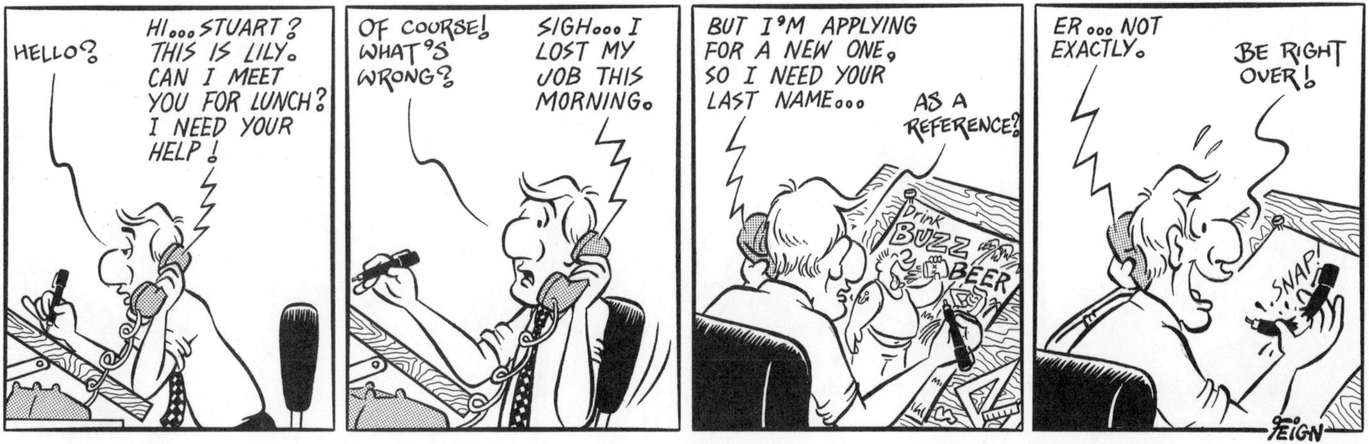
HELLO?
HI... STUART? THIS IS LILY. CAN I MEET YOU FOR LUNCH? I NEED YOUR HELP!
OF COURSE! WHAT'S WRONG?
SIGH... I LOST MY JOB THIS MORNING.
BUT I'M APPLYING FOR A NEW ONE, SO I NEED YOUR LAST NAME...
AS A REFERENCE?
Drink BUZZ BEER
ER... NOT EXACTLY.
BE RIGHT OVER!
SNAP!
FEIGN

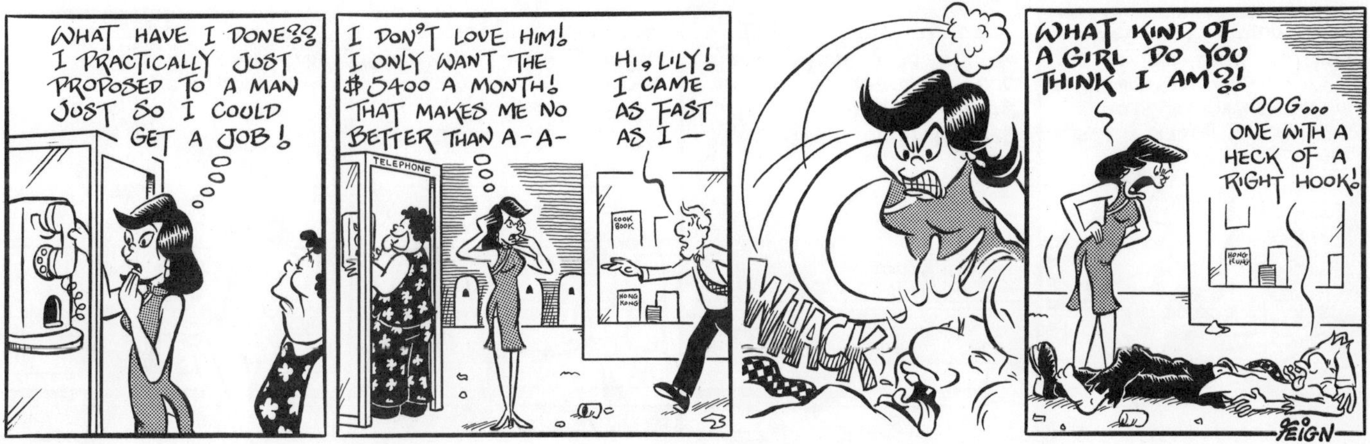
WHAT HAVE I DONE?? I PRACTICALLY JUST PROPOSED TO A MAN JUST SO I COULD GET A JOB!
I DON'T LOVE HIM! I ONLY WANT THE $5400 A MONTH! THAT MAKES ME NO BETTER THAN A-A-
TELEPHONE
HI, LILY! I CAME AS FAST AS I —
COOK BOOK
HONG KONG
WHACK
WHAT KIND OF A GIRL DO YOU THINK I AM?!
OOG... ONE WITH A HECK OF A RIGHT HOOK!
FEIGN

SORRY, STUART, I DIDN'T MEAN TO HURT YOU. I'M JUST MAD AT THE WORLD.
THAT'S OKAY. YOU KNOW WHAT THEY SAY: "YOU ONLY HURT THE ONE YOU LOVE."
OH, REALLY??
LIKE I JUST SAID~ I DIDN'T MEAN TO HURT YOU!
FEIGN

...SO THE BANK SAID THEY'D HIRE ME IF I COULD SOMEHOW OBTAIN A FOREIGN PASSPORT WITHIN A WEEK! ISN'T THAT CRAZY?
AIWA
CANON
WHAT DO THEY EXPECT ME TO DO? MARRY ANY OLD FOREIGNER FOR THE SAKE OF A LOUSY SECRETARIAL POSITION?!
PILOT
YOU KNOW, I EVEN THOUGHT ABOUT MARRYING YOU, JUST TO GET THE JOB!
CAN YOU IMAGINE ANYTHING SO RIDICULOUS??
I'M TRYING! I'M TRYING!
FEIGN

I CAN'T TAKE IT ANYMORE! MEN ARE RUINING MY LIFE!!
MY FATHER AND BROTHER TREAT ME LIKE DIRT, MY BOSS FIRES ME AFTER SEVEN YEARS WITHOUT A WORD OF THANKS, AND NOW THIS MAN AT THE BANK MAKES SILLY CONDITIONS BEFORE HE'LL HIRE ME!
Grrrrrr...
I HATE MEN!!
ER... WHERE DO I FIT IN THERE...?
SORRY, I DIDN'T MEAN YOU, STUART. I WAS TALKING ABOUT MEN!
G.O. FEIGN

YOU KNOW, I'M ENJOYING NOT WORKING. IN FACT, I WISH I NEVER HAD TO WORK AGAIN!
WELL, LILY, THERE IS A WAY YOU'D NEVER HAVE TO DO ANY WORK EVER AGAIN, YET HAVE ALL YOUR NEEDS TAKEN CARE OF...
YOU'RE RIGHT, STUART. I'LL DO IT!
GREAT! I'LL CALL MY MOTHER!
HUH? WHY WOULD YOUR MOTHER CARE IF I GET A CIVIL SERVICE JOB?
G.O. FEIGN

7 All That Glitters

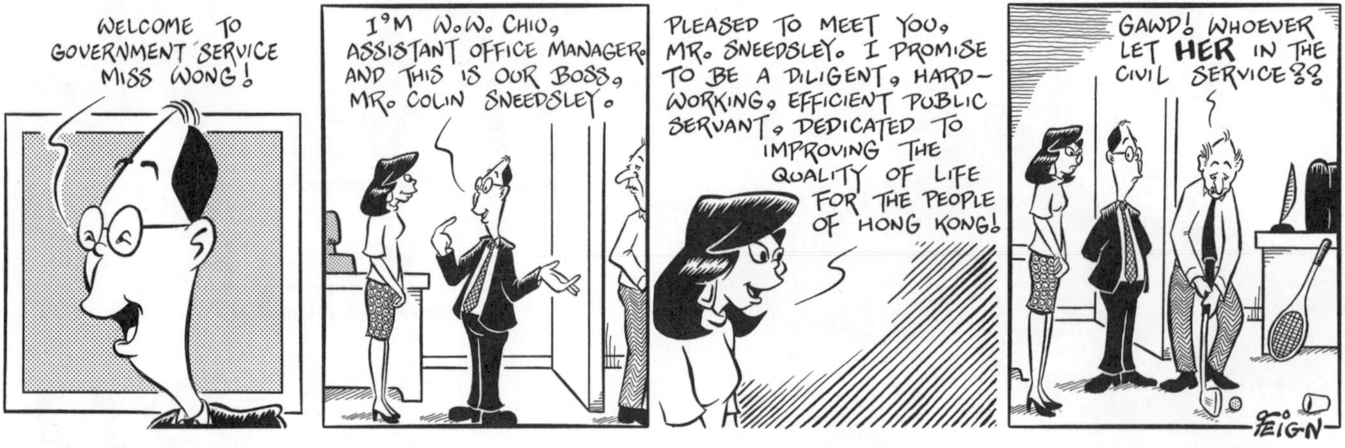
WELCOME TO GOVERNMENT SERVICE MISS WONG!
I'M W.W. CHIU, ASSISTANT OFFICE MANAGER. AND THIS IS OUR BOSS, MR. COLIN SNEEDSLEY.
PLEASED TO MEET YOU, MR. SNEEDSLEY. I PROMISE TO BE A DILIGENT, HARD-WORKING, EFFICIENT PUBLIC SERVANT, DEDICATED TO IMPROVING THE QUALITY OF LIFE FOR THE PEOPLE OF HONG KONG!
GAWD! WHOEVER LET HER IN THE CIVIL SERVICE??
FEIGN

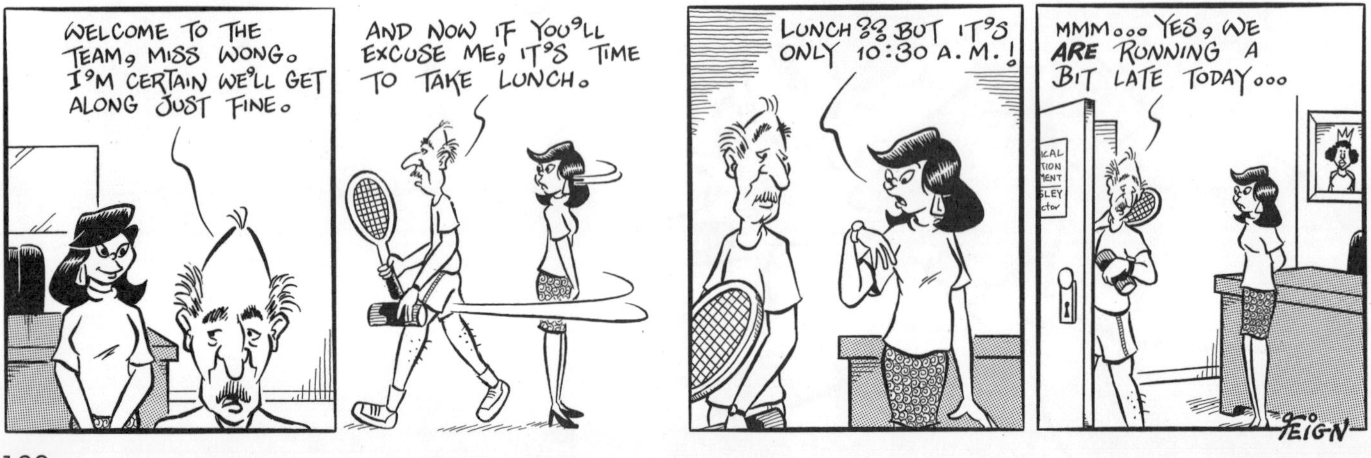
WELCOME TO THE TEAM, MISS WONG. I'M CERTAIN WE'LL GET ALONG JUST FINE.
AND NOW IF YOU'LL EXCUSE ME, IT'S TIME TO TAKE LUNCH.
LUNCH?? BUT IT'S ONLY 10:30 A.M.!
MMM... YES, WE ARE RUNNING A BIT LATE TODAY...
FEIGN

MR. CHIU, WHICH OPERATING SYSTEM DO WE USE ON THIS COMPUTER?
WE USE SEVERAL. BUT THIS ONE IS THE MOST POPULAR.
INSERT THE DISKETTE, WAIT FOR THESE WORDS, THEN SELECT 1, 2 OR 3...
... AND WHEN THE SPACE ALIENS START SHOOTING, YOU TURN YOUR ROCKET WITH THIS, FIRE WITH...
BLIP! BEEP!
FEIGN

MR. CHIU, JUST WHAT DOES THIS GOVERNMENT DEPARTMENT DO?
WE'RE IN CHARGE OF THE RUBBISH TREATMENT PROGRAMME.
OH, YOU MEAN LIKE SEWAGE DISPOSAL, COMPOSTING, WATER OXYGENATION...
NO, WE TAKE ALL THE ROSY GOVERNMENT REPORTS ABOUT THE ENVIRONMENT AND FIND STATISTICS TO MATCH THEM!
OH, **THAT** KIND OF RUBBISH...
BEAUTIFUL TOLO HARBOUR
FEIGN

UH, MR. CHIU, I'VE FINISHED TYPING THIS REPORT. NOW WHAT DO I DO?
THAT'S UP TO YOU.
HERE IN THE CIVIL SERVICE, ONE MUST RELY ON ONE'S OWN INITIATIVE IN DECIDING HOW TO MAKE THE BEST USE OF ONE'S TIME.
WHAT ARE MY CHOICES?
WELL, ANNIE HERE KNITS, JOHNSON LIKES COMPUTER GAMES, THERESA HAS HER WALKMAN...
FEIGN

TIME TO GO.
SEE YOU TOMORROW!
STATISTIC
EVALUATI
SUBJECT
YOU'RE GOING HOME? IT'S NOT EVEN 4:00!
SO?
SO?! IN MY LAST JOB, I WORKED 9-6 WITH ONLY AN HOUR FOR LUNCH!
YEAH, I HEARD THEY DO THINGS LIKE THAT IN THE PRIVATE SECTOR.
POOR THING! LUCKY YOU JOINED US!
STATISTI
EVALUATI
SUBJECT
FEIGN

LEI LEI, HOW IS YOUR NEW JOB?
SIGH... OH, MOTHER...
IT'S OKAY, I GUESS. THERE'S NOTHING VERY STIMULATING ABOUT IT, HARDLY ANYTHING TO DO...
THE BIGGEST CHALLENGE IS FIGURING OUT HOW TO KILL TIME BEFORE GOING HOME. IN FACT, I'M BORED TO TEARS!
WAH! THINK THEY HIRE WAITERS IN THE CIVIL SERVICE?
FEIGN

OH, MOTHER, I'M SO DEPRESSED!
I DON'T ENJOY MY NEW JOB, ALL MY FRIENDS HAVE EITHER MARRIED OR EMIGRATED, YOU'RE ALL TALKING ABOUT LEAVING TOO, AND THE ONLY MAN IN MY LIFE IS A GOOFY GWAILO I HARDLY LIKE!
I'M SO UNHAPPY! BOO HOO HOO...
THERE, THERE, HAPPINESS ISN'T EVERYTHING...
I MEAN, LOOK AT ME! I'VE NEVER BEEN HAPPY, BUT I'M HAPPY!
FEIGN

LEI LEI, LET'S HAVE YOUR FORTUNE TOLD.
ALRIGHT. BUT HOW DO WE CHOOSE A FORTUNE TELLER?
WELL... CONSISTENCY IS MORE IMPORTANT THAN ACCURACY.
WHAT DO YOU MEAN?
INSTEAD OF RISKING FINDING ONE WHO MAY BE RIGHT AND MAY BE WRONG...
...FIND ONE WHO IS **ALWAYS** WRONG AND BELIEVE THE OPPOSITE!
FORMER EMPLOYEE of ROYAL OBSERVATORY
FEIGN

AH! YOUR MARRIAGE LINE IS QUITE GOOD!
YOU'LL BE MARRIED BY THE END OF NEXT YEAR TO A MAN WHO DEARLY LOVES YOU.
I SEE A MAN LIGHT IN COMPLEXION, THIN, WITH A BIG NOSE...
AND VERY HANDSOME, CHARMING AND WEALTHY.
WHEW!
FEIGN

THAT WILL BE $100, MISS!
$100?? BUT WE AGREED ON $70!
YES, BUT THAT WAS BEFORE I PREDICTED...
...THAT YOU'D MARRY A GWAILO!
FEIGN

CHEN, OUR NEW CLIENT, "HONKIE" TOOTHPASTE, NEEDS A NEW IMAGE, A SPOKESPERSON TO REPRESENT THEM.
HONKIE
SOMEBODY KNOWN FOR THEIR TEETH, EH? HOW ABOUT ALAN TAM?
TOO EXPENSIVE.
ELSIE TU?
NO FOREIGNERS!
I'VE GOT IT! THE MOST FAMOUS SET OF PEARLY WHITES IN THE TERRITORY!
HONKIE
USE HONKIE TOOTH PASTE
Official Toothpaste OF THE NEW CHINA NEWS AGENCY
FEIGN

SIR, OUR CLIENT IS HONOURED TO HAVE YOU AS THEIR SPOKESMAN.
HONKIE
THIS COULD BE THE WAVE OF THE FUTURE FOR HONG KONG ADVERTISING! A TRUE CONVERGENCE OF SOCIALISM AND CAPITALISM!
FAUST & ASSOCIATES ADVERTISING
FA
I UNDERSTAND. BUT WHAT DOES YOUR PRODUCT DO?
WELL, IT CLEANS YOUR TEETH AND FRESHENS YOUR BREATH.
AH, YOU MEAN "ONE TOOTHPASTE, TWO SYSTEMS!"
QUICK! WRITE THAT DOWN!
FEIGN

SEE THAT? THAT'S ROUGH UGLY FOREIGN BOURGEOIS CONTAMINATON.
...BEFORE, ONLY YOUR PARTY CADRE COULD CHIP IT OFF.
...BUT NOW THERE'S IMPROVED "HONKIE" TOOTHPASTE, NEWLY MODERNISED WITH FOUR IDEOLOGICAL SAFEGUARDS!
HONKIE
HONKIE
TOOTH PASTE
...LET A HUNDRED INCISORS BLOSSOM! CONVERGE WITH "HONKIE" TOOTHPASTE...FOR THE STABILITY AND PROSPERITY OF YOUR TEETH!
FEIGN

WHAT'S OUR POINT-OF-SALES TIE-IN TO THE HONKIE "ONE TOOTHPASTE TWO SYSTEMS" PROMOTION?
WELL, WE HAVE PEOPLE IN ALL THE SHOPS PUSHING THE PRODUCT THE SAME WAY THE LEFTISTS PUSH THEIR POLITICAL VIEWS.
YOU MEAN WITH LITERATURE AND SLOGANS?
NO, BY BULLYING AND HECKLING PEOPLE WHO BUY OTHER BRANDS!

CHEN, WHAT ARE THE SURVEY RESULTS SINCE THE LAUNCH OF THE HONKIE "ONE TOOTHPASTE TWO SYSTEMS" CAMPAIGN?
GOOD NEWS AND BAD NEWS, SIR.
THE GOOD NEWS...?
JUST AS WE EXPECTED— SALES FIGURES ARE CLEARLY LINKED TO PUBLIC CONFIDENCE IN THE FUTURE OF HONG KONG.
THE BAD NEWS?
SALES HAVE FALLEN THROUGH THE FLOOR. THE COMPANY'S GONE BANKRUPT.
OOPS...
ZZZZ

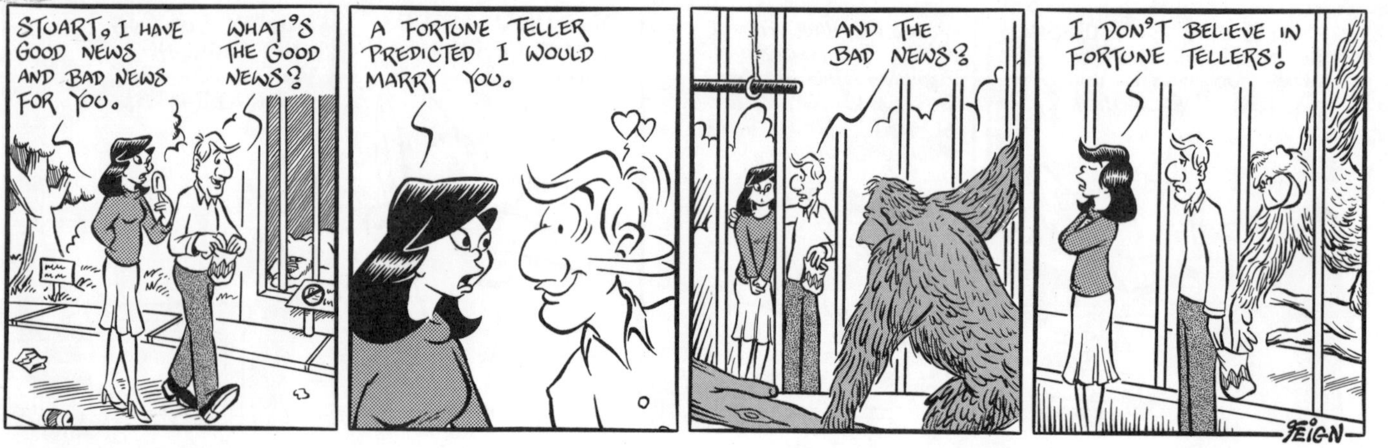
STUART, I HAVE GOOD NEWS AND BAD NEWS FOR YOU.
WHAT'S THE GOOD NEWS?
A FORTUNE TELLER PREDICTED I WOULD MARRY YOU.
AND THE BAD NEWS?
I DON'T BELIEVE IN FORTUNE TELLERS!
FEIGN

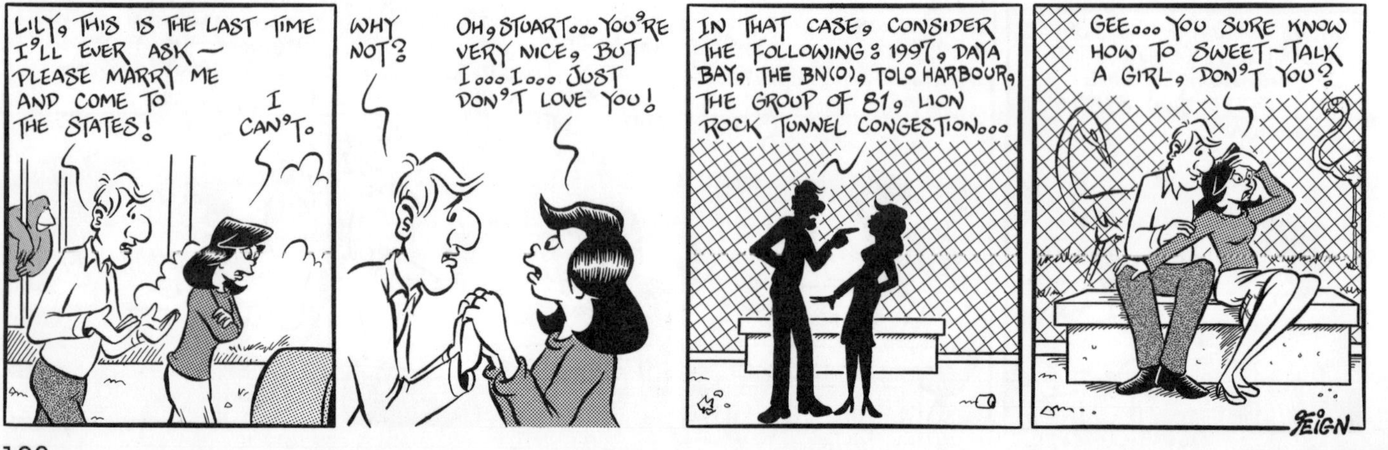
LILY, THIS IS THE LAST TIME I'LL EVER ASK — PLEASE MARRY ME AND COME TO THE STATES!
I CAN'T.
WHY NOT?
OH, STUART... YOU'RE VERY NICE, BUT I... I... JUST DON'T LOVE YOU!
IN THAT CASE, CONSIDER THE FOLLOWING: 1997, DAYA BAY, THE BN(O), TOLO HARBOUR, THE GROUP OF 81, LION ROCK TUNNEL CONGESTION...
GEE... YOU SURE KNOW HOW TO SWEET-TALK A GIRL, DON'T YOU?
FEIGN

HOW CAN YOU EXPECT A MARRIAGE BETWEEN US TO WORK?? WE'RE SO... SO... DIFFERENT!
THINK OF IT AS "CONVERGENCE". ENGAGEMENT IS OUR JOINT DECLARATION, MARRIAGE IS OUR BASIC LAW...
WE'D HAVE "ONE MARRIAGE TWO SYSTEMS" — EACH WITH COMPLETE AUTONOMY IN MATTERS OF ECONOMICS AND LIFESTYLE...
... AS LONG AS WE BOTH DON'T GET INVOLVED IN FOREIGN AFFAIRS!
I'LL THINK ABOUT IT.
FEIGN

SO HOW ABOUT IT, LILY — WILL YOU MARRY ME?
UNDER ONE CONDITION...
14K?! WHAT KIND OF A GIRL DO YOU THINK I AM??
ONE OBVIOUSLY BRED IN HONG KONG.
FEIGN

THANK YOU FOR THE RING, STUART. IT'S BEAUTIFUL!
I CAN'T WAIT TO SHOW MY FAMILY! I'LL CHERISH IT FOREVER! I'LL—
OH MY GOSH! GOLD JUST JUMPED 58 POINTS!!
GOLD PRICE
BUY 4481
SELL 4501
SIGH... YOU CAN TRY TO TAKE THE WOMAN OUT OF HONG KONG, BUT YOU CAN'T TAKE HONG KONG OUT OF THE WOMAN...
JACKSON JEWELLERY
FEIGN

WE'RE LOOKING FOR AN ENGAGEMENT RING.
I SEE. AND WHY ARE YOU GETTING MARRIED?
WHAT DIFFERENCE DOES IT MAKE?
WELL, IF YOU'RE MARRYING FOR LOVE, WE HAVE THESE TASTEFUL DIAMOND-STUDDED BANDS...
IF IT'S FOR MONEY, WE HAVE GAUDY MULTI-JEWELED SETTINGS. AND FOR PEOPLE LIKE YOU, WE HAVE THE "1997 SPECIAL"...
...SO THAT ALL HER FRIENDS CAN KNOW WHICH PASSPORT SHE'S MARRYING!
U.K.
USA
CAN.
AUS.
N.Z.
FRANCE
PORT.
SWEDEN
FEIGN

STUART, BEFORE WE CAN GET ENGAGED, YOU'LL HAVE TO MEET MY FAMILY.
G·3·6·9·12·15
B-BUT YOU SAID YOUR FATHER DESPISES GWAILO! WON'T HE BE RATHER... UNACCOMODATING?
DON'T WORRY. I CALLED AND TOLD HIM YOU'RE COMING. HE'S PROBABLY JUST GETTING DRESSED!
BZZZ
FEIGN
HI! I'M STUART WRIGHT. PLEASED TO—
YOU DIDN'T TELL ME YOUR FATHER WAS A KONG FU EXPERT!
YOU DIDN'T ASK.
FEIGN

WHY DOES YOUR FATHER HATE GWAILO?
HE SAYS MOST WESTERNERS IN HONG KONG ARE ARROGANT, OVERPAID, SELF-INDULGENT, RUDE, GREEDY, ALCOHOLIC, SHORT-TEMPERED, ELITIST, LINGUISTIC AND CULTURAL CHAUVINIST MERCENARIES!
SO? AREN'T YOU GOING TO REPLY?
REPLY?? I COULDN'T HAVE SAID IT BETTER MYSELF!
FEIGN

YOU ARE ENGLAND MAN?
NO, I'M AMERICAN.
AH, SAME! PUT DOWN CHINESE!
NOT AT ALL! IN FACT, HONG KONG AND THE USA HAVE A LOT IN COMMON!
JUST LIKE HONG KONG, WE WERE A BRITISH COLONY FOR EXACTLY 156 YEARS! THEN THE BRITISH FINALLY LEFT AND WE GAINED INDEPENDENCE!
INDEPENDENCE? AND BEIJING NOT OBJECT??
FEIGN

Panel 1: "Hey, Gwailo, want a cigarette?" "No, thanks, I don't smoke."

Panel 4: "Now you do!" "Cough! Hack! East is East — gasp! And West is West... but smokers will be smokers!"

Panel 5: "Lily, I don't think your family likes me." "How can you say that?"

Panel 6: "Well, your father threw me to the floor, your brother blows smoke in my face..."

Panel 7: "...and your mother doesn't speak to me!" "Oh, don't worry. It's really nothing..."

Panel 8: "...compared to what they SAID they were going to do to you!"

113

8 Farewell, My Lily

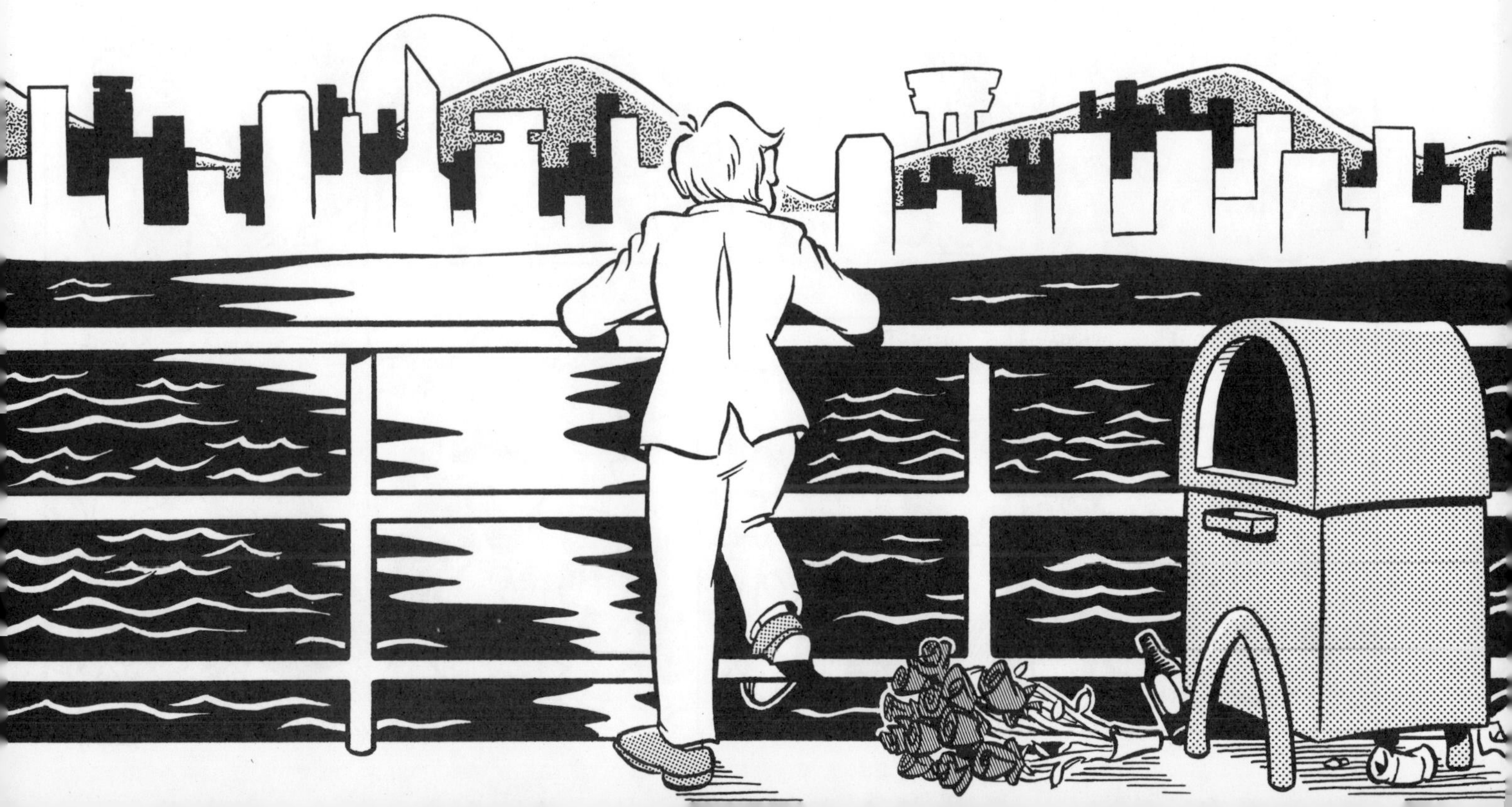

EMBER
WAH! I'VE BEEN ACCEPTED FOR IMMIGRATION TO CANADA!
PORTNOY'S COMPL
Philip Roth
YOU?? WHY WOULD THEY WANT SOMEONE LIKE YOU??
I HAVE A HIGH PRIORITY PROFESSION. 10 POINTS!
WAITER?! HIGH PRIORITY?? BUT IT SHOULDN'T BE HARD TO FIND COMPETENT, EFFICIENT WAITERS IN CANADA!
YOU'RE RIGHT, IT ISN'T.
...BUT SURLY WAITERS ARE HARD TO FIND!
CANADA
Sir/Madam: You have been accepted for immigration; job category 319: WAITER, SURLY, LAZY
FEIGN

HEY, EVERYBODY! WE'RE ALL MOVING TO CANADA!
NO, WE'RE NOT!
I DIDN'T EVEN APPLY!
OH, WE APPLIED FOR YOU.
HOW COULD YOU?? AND ANYWAY I DIDN'T GO TO THE INTERVIEW.
DON'T WORRY...
...I TOOK CARE OF THAT FOR YOU, TOO!
Application
WONG
LILY
F 26
FEIGN

WHAT CITY IN CANADA DID YOU APPLY FOR?
UH... LET'S SEE... WAN-GO-WA...
OH, VANCOUVER! I'VE HEARD THAT'S A NICE CITY— UNCROWDED, QUIET, CLEAN, THE PEOPLE FRIENDLY AND POLITE...
OH YEAH? WELL I HEARD JUST THE OPPOSITE!
WHAT DID YOU HEAR?
THAT A LOT OF HONG KONG PEOPLE LIVE THERE!
FEIGN

MOTHER! FATHER! IT'S CRAZY, MOVING TO CANADA! YOU'VE LIVED HERE YOUR WHOLE LIVES! YOU DON'T SPEAK ENGLISH!
MUK TAO
I CAN SEE IT NOW: YOU'LL LIVE IN CHINATOWN, HAVE ONLY CHINESE FRIENDS, HEAR CHINESE RADIO, WORK IN A CHINESE RESTAURANT...
...TOTALLY CUT OFF FROM THE MAINSTREAM CULTURE! YOU'LL BE JUST LIKE THE GWAILO HERE IN HONG KONG!
YOU MEAN THEY'RE GIVING US FREE LUXURY FLATS AND HOME LEAVE TOO??
RACING NEWS
FEIGN

MR. SNEEDSLEY, MY FAMILY IS EMIGRATING, SO I'M AFRAID I HAVE TO GIVE YOU MY NOTICE.
YACHTING
I GUESS THAT MAKES ME A "LAME DUCK" SECRETARY! HA HA!
YOU ARE NOT TO USE THAT TERM, MISS WONG! THERE ARE NO "LAME DUCKS" IN THE HONG KONG GOVERNMENT!
THE NEW CATCHPHRASE AROUND HERE IS THAT WE ARE TIGERS!
TIGERS? BUT I THOUGHT TIGERS ARE NOCTURNAL PREDATORS WHO LURK AT NIGHT...
... AND SLEEP ALL DAY!
BEAUTIFUL METAPHOR, ISN'T IT?
TISTICAL
VALUATION
BSECTION
FEIGN

FOLLOWING THE LEAD OF THE CHIEF SECRETARY, FROM NOW ON ALL GOVERNMENT DEPARTMENTS ARE TO REACT TO CRITICISM LIKE TIGERS!
RING!
COLIN SNEEDSLEY...
HELLO, THIS IS THE TWELFTH NUMBER I'VE CALLED! WON'T THE GOVERNMENT DO SOMETHING ABOUT THE CHEMICAL LEAK AT—
ROAR
WAH! SURE BEATS HAVING TO ACTUALLY DO ANYTHING!
RIGHT... YAWN... TIME FOR THIS TIGER TO TAKE A LITTLE CAT NAP.
FEIGN

ARE WE GOVERNMENT EMPLOYEES SUPPOSED TO REACT LIKE TIGERS TO ALL CRITICISM?
THAT DEPENDS.
STICAL
ATION
ECTION
IF THE CRITICISM IS FROM THE PUBLIC OR LEGISLATIVE COUNCILLORS, OF COURSE WE ROAR LIKE FEROCIOUS WILDCATS!
AND IF IT'S FROM RICH INDUSTRIALISTS OR BEIJING?
WE MEW LIKE KITTENS.
FEIGN

WELL, I'M SORRY YOU'RE LEAVING, MISS WONG. ALLOW ME TO PRESENT YOU WITH THIS TEN-YEAR DISTINGUISHED SERVICE PLAQUE.
STATISTIC
EVALUATI
SUBSECTI
HK
10
TEN YEARS? BUT I'VE ONLY WORKED HERE SIX WEEKS!
I KNOW. BUT IN YOUR SIX WEEKS ON THE JOB...
...YOU DID AS MUCH WORK AS MOST CIVIL SERVANTS WOULD DO IN TEN YEARS!
STATISTICA
EVALUATIO
SUBSECTIO
FEIGN

HI, LILY! WHERE DO YOU WANT TO EAT TONIGHT? THAI, IND~
STUART, I'M EMIGRATING.
YOU'RE W~WHAT??
I SAID I'M EMIGRATING.
OH.
CAN YOU AT LEAST WAIT UNTIL AFTER DINNER?
ALRIGHT. BUT WE BETTER HURRY.
FEIGN

LILY, I THOUGHT WE'RE ENGAGED!! REMEMBER, I PROMISED OUR MARRIAGE WILL BE JUST LIKE THE BASIC LAW...
ONE MARRIAGE TWO SYSTEMS, COMPLETE AUTONOMY EXCEPT FOR FOREIGN AFFAIRS.
I KNOW, STUART. AND MY RESPONSE IS THE SAME AS HONG KONG PEOPLE'S RESPONSE TO THE BASIC LAW...
TOTAL LACK OF INTEREST!
MENU
FEIGN

I THOUGHT YOU DIDN'T WANT TO EMIGRATE!
I DON'T! I LOVE HONG KONG! THIS IS MY HOME!
BUT MY FAMILY INSISTS ON GOING. I HAVE NO CHOICE.
OY! CAN'T YOU JUST ONCE NOT BE THE GOOD LITTLE CHINESE GIRL??
ASSERT YOUR INDEPENDENCE! BE AN INDIVIDUAL! DO SOMETHING FOR YOURSELF!
LIKE WHAT?
LIKE MARRY ME.
FEIGN

LILY, PLEASE DON'T LEAVE! I-I NEED YOU! I I LOVE YOU! PLEASE MARRY ME, FOR GOD'S SAKE!
OH, STUART. I'M SO SICK AND TIRED OF YOU ASKING ME TO MARRY YOU.
WHAT CAN I SAY TO MAKE YOU STOP ASKING THAT QUESTION??
"YES."
FEIGN

SNIFF! WE MAY NEVER SEE EACH OTHER AGAIN.
B-BUT BEFORE YOU GO, WOULD... WOULD YOU GIVE ME JUST ONE LAST LITTLE...
WHACK!
THANKS, LILY. YOUR FACE WILL ALWAYS BE IN MY HEART.
YOUR TEETH WILL ALWAYS BE IN MY WRIST!
FEIGN

SIGH... SHE'S GONE...
seway Bay
tation
I GUESS IT WASN'T MEANT TO BE.
I'LL JUST HAVE TO FIND SOMEONE ELSE. THE SAME WAY I FOUND LILY.
PARDON ME, MISS. MIND IF I LEAN HERE?
FEIGN

Epilogue

RUDY, WHERE'S THAT ACCEPTANCE LETTER FROM CANADA? I NEED TO SHOW IT TO MY BOSS!
RIGHT THERE.
RACING
WHAT?!! THIS ISN'T AN ACCEPTANCE LETTER!!
WHAT ARE YOU TALKING ABOUT?
CAN'T YOU READ?? "Dear Mr. Wong and family, you will be accepted for immigration to Canada..."
I KNOW!
"...over my dead body! signed, Commissioner for Canada"
YOU MEAN I SHOULDN'T HAVE SENT HIM A CONDOLENCE CARD?
RACING
FEIGN
SINCE WE'RE NOT MOVING TO CANADA, LET'S GO TO RETURN THE PLANE TICKETS.
NO NEED. I NEVER GOT THEM.
STAR FERRY SECOND CLAS
EXACT FARE 50c
WHAT?? I THOUGHT YOU TOOK ALL OUR MONEY OUT OF THE BANK THIS MORNING TO GO DOWN AND PAY FOR THEM!
ER... WELL... YES AND NO...
BET
LET'S ENJOY FROM BEAT, WHETHER
OH WELL... I DIDN'T WANT TO LEAVE HONG KONG ANYWAY...!
FEIGN

> This sceptred isle,
> this other Eden,
> This precious stone set
> in the silver sea,

> Which serves it in the
> office of a wall,
> Against the envy of
> less happier lands;

This nurse, this teeming womb of money'd kings,

This blessed plot, this earth, this realm, This Hong Kong...

Smoke WHEEZE

Apologies to W.S.!

FEIGN

GLOSSARY

For those new to Hong Kong, unfamiliar with Hong Kong, and that 90% of the expatriate population who've lived in Hong Kong for years and years, and still don't know a damn thing about what's going on.

Ah-Ba	"father" (affectionate term)
amah	house servant; what people think any Asian woman is when she's seen with a foreign male
Basic Law	Mini-constitution for post-1997 Hong Kong, currently being drafted by a select group of people and being ignored by the rest
BN(O)	British National (Overseas) so-called "passport"; useful for shooing away cockroaches. Britain uses it for shooing away Hong Kong people.
catty	Chinese unit of measure: approximately 1⅓ pounds weight . . . unless you're a foreigner, in which case it's more like 6 ounces.
Chief Secretary	Hong Kong's second-in-command, renowned for trying to change the government's image from lame duck to tiger.
Leslie Cheung	second-most popular male singer in Hong Kong
choi sum	my favourite Chinese vegetable
congee	rice porridge; eaten during breakfast, childhood, and prison terms
daai paai dong	street-side restaurants, currently being legislated out of existence by priggish civil servants who'd like to see Hong Kong have all the charm and colour of a parking lot
Daya Bay	site of China's first nuclear power plant, just a few miles upwind of Hong Kong
faan gwai lo	"foreign devil man"; a more belligerent term than "gwai lo"
fung shui	"wind and water"; Chinese traditional belief in good fortune in relation to geographical alignment of structures
Group of 81	group of Basic Law drafters and consultants to whom "democracy" is almost as dirty a word as "profit loss", "workers' rights" or "ecology"
gwai	"ghost" or "devil"
gwaipoh	female gwailo
gwailo	"devil man"; generic or belligerent (depending on the tone of voice) term for foreigners
Hung Hom	low-rent district in Kowloon
Joint Declaration	1984 pact over Hong Kong's future, in which China declared that Britain should hand over the joint.
Martin Lee	Elected member of Legco and outspoken champion of democracy, free speech, human rights, and everything else Legco is always passing laws against.
Legco	Legislative Council; Hong Kong's "parliament", dominated by unelected government-appointees (see "Shoe shiner")

Mai Po Marsh	wildlife preserve located in the northern New Territories; home or migratory stopover for over 200 species of birds
MTR	Mass Transit Railway; Hong Kong's underground rail system, with an emphasis on the "mass"
Anita Mui	most popular female singer in Hong Kong
Ocker	Australian for "Australian"
The Peak	Breeding ground for the rich, the overpaid, and the civil service
Shoe shiner	Chinese way of calling one a sycophant or "ass-kisser" (see Legco)
Alan Tam	most popular male singer in Hong Kong
Toló Harbour	Possibly the most polluted body of water on earth. So polluted that even the E.Coli bacteria gasp for breath
triad	Chinese gang; historically secret societies of patriotic revolutionary zealots, they have mostly devolved into organised criminal gangs
Elsie Tu	long time English resident and politician; known for her toothy, but charming, grin
Wai	Cantonese way to answer the telephone
Xinhua	New China News Agency; China's de facto embassy (and thus Hong Kong's de facto government)
14K	major criminal triad gang in Hong Kong
1997	the year the British finally leave Hong Kong. By then, everyone else will have already left.

ABOUT THE AUTHOR

Casting aside promising careers as a doctor and/or lawyer at the age of ten, the author then proceeded to further disappoint his mother by meandering through a series of other professions, including teacher, ice cream maker, rock-and-roll violinist, and petrol station toilet janitor, until one day a heavenly voice spake and hath said: "Let there be cartoons!"

Since that time he has drawn caricatures in Hawaii, animation in Hollywood, and cartoons for numerous magazines, books and toy designs. "The World of Lily Wong" comic strip appeared daily in Hong Kong from November 1986 through May 1995, when it was abruptly terminated in an apparent act of political censorship by the *South China Morning Post*. Lily has also been a daily feature in Malaysia's *New Straits Times* and has appeared in publications around the world.

Larry Feign lives on Lantau Island in Hong Kong with his wife Cathy (no, she is not Lily Wong) and two perfect children, Ivan and Annika. He has published nine other books. Buy them.

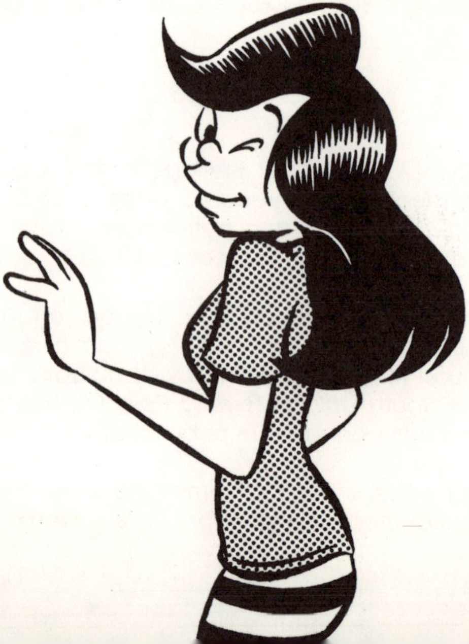